Remarks from

"The short fiction I love best knows h.... .. .., .
prefer not to.' It takes the page as a space to refuse what tends to
be, unzipping barriers. This collection gathers stories from voices
throwing rice at the moment the essential and the original meet."

—TRACY O'NEILL, 2020 judge and
author of *Quotients* and *The Hopeful*

"I love the stories we picked for this collection. I love their passion,
invention, and wildness. I love that these are the artists' first published stories. Your first published story never quite gives up its
place in the mind. It was the first one *chosen*—hooray! And yet
there is always the nagging doubt ('Is it actually good?') and here
we are, celebrating, saying, 'Yes, yes, it is good, so *so* good!'"

—DEB OLIN UNFERTH, 2020 judge and
author of *Barn 8* and *Wait Till You See Me Dance*

"The stories and writers here represent a wide range of voices at the
levels of ethnicity, gender, and style. Many carry a very quiet confidence that is refreshing in our harried world, and I feel certain that
we will see these authors' names in print again soon."

—NAFISSA THOMPSON-SPIRES, 2020 judge and
author of *Heads of the Colored People*

"I was really inspired by what I saw here—not just the beautiful
weirdness of the writers and their work, but the fact that the stories
were published. It made me feel so hopeful."

—CARMEN MARIA MACHADO, 2019 judge and
author of *In the Dream House* and *Her Body and Other Parties*

"I was so blown away by the pieces we chose for this collection—there was a wonderful array of different styles and approaches in the submissions we received, but each of the stories we ended up choosing had something startlingly alive and bracingly imaginative within it. You can tell that these are writers working with total dedication to gift these fictive worlds to their readers, to make these surprising, vivid scenarios real. I am so wildly enthusiastic about what these writers are going to do next—and in reading this anthology, you get to say you've followed their entire career, from the very first short story on! You can't beat that."

—ALEXANDRA KLEEMAN, 2018 judge and author of
Intimations and *You Too Can Have a Body Like Mine*

"When I sit down with a short story, I'm hoping to be surprised, or unnerved, or waylaid. I want to feel that something is at stake: in the language and structure, in the emotional lives of the characters, in the consequences of their actions. The best stories are almost otherworldly in their dimensions, as if I have opened a small suitcase left on my front door, only to find three geese, a small child, a jewel thief, and her mother emerging. The stories here delighted and surprised and moved me—I'm so very, very glad that I got to read them and that now you do too."

—KELLY LINK, 2017 judge, 2018 MacArthur Fellow,
and author of *Get in Trouble*

"There were very well written stories that didn't end up on the final list, edged out by the magnitude of feeling and creativity contained in the final twelve. I was particularly struck by the authors' ability to hit it out of the park, first time up. When I read I'm always (like it or not) guessing what's going to happen at the end of the line, the scene, on the plot level. The stories we chose were those that forced me, a relentless overthinker, to stop thinking.

"Amy Hempel's first short story was 'In the Cemetery Where Al Jolson Is Buried.' That story is great, and contains many of the elements she's famous for, but it is not like most of her stories. It's way longer, for one, and more traditional. As if she was only able to peel her inhibitions as she wrote more and more. I'm excited for these authors to participate in that same kind of peeling that helps voice grow more substantial, and I hope this honor gives them the confidence to get weirder and weirder, stronger and stronger."

—MARIE-HELENE BERTINO, 2017 judge and
author of *Parakeet* and *2 A.M. at The Cat's Pajamas*

"A lot of people talk about how so many short stories are becoming too workshopped, too MFA, too a certain kind of story. And I can say, after reading all the entries here, they are wrong. There are so many stories being told that are extraordinary and unexpected. I fretted over picking only twelve. But the stories that won were all stories that astounded us all." —NINA McCONIGLEY, 2017 judge and
author of *Cowboys and East Indians*

Praise for PEN America
Best Debut Short Stories 2019

"These stories all share a sense of necessity and urgency . . . What consistently runs through all 12 entries in *PEN America Best Debut Short Stories 2019* is the promise of clear new voices, powerful testimonies, and unique perspectives to assure us that even in our current dark times there will always be the short narrative to take us back into the light." —CHRISTOPHER JOHN STEPHENS, *PopMatters*

"Prominent issues of social justice and cultural strife are woven thematically throughout 12 stories. Stories of prison reform, the immigrant experience, and the aftermath of sexual assault make the book a vivid time capsule that will guide readers back into the ethos of 2019 for generations to come . . . Each story displays a mastery of the form, sure to inspire readers to seek out further writing from these adept authors and publications." —*Booklist*

Praise for PEN America
Best Debut Short Stories 2018

"The PEN America contest for outstanding debut fiction returns with a second annual anthology of remarkable prose. This year's submissions were judged by an all-star trio of fiction writers: Jodi Angel, Lesley Nneka Arimah, and Alexandra Kleeman. Once again, the gathered contest winners are uniquely gifted writers whose stories represent literature's bright tomorrow. The pieces showcase a wide breadth of human experiences, representing numerous racial, ethnic, and cultural identities . . . Sharp, engrossing, and sure to leave readers excited about the future of the craft." —*Booklist*

"These dozen stories tend to the dark side, with rare moments of humor in a moody fictive landscape; they're thus just right for their time . . . A pleasure for fans of short fiction and a promise of good things to come from this year's roster of prizewinners."

—*Kirkus Reviews*

Praise for PEN America
Best Debut Short Stories 2017

"Urgent fiction, from breakout talents."   —*Booklist*

"A great overview of some of the year's most interesting fiction."
                                                    —*Vol. 1 Brooklyn*

BEST DEBUT SHORT STORIES 2020

EDITED BY
YUKA IGARASHI

JUDGES
TRACY O'NEILL
NAFISSA THOMPSON-SPIRES
DEB OLIN UNFERTH

THE PEN AMERICA DAU PRIZE

CATAPULT   NEW YORK

Please see Permissions on page 233 for individual credits.

ISBN: 978-1-64622-022-9

ISSN: 2691-6533 (print)
ISSN: 2691-655X (online)

Cover design by Strick&Williams

Printed in the United States of America
10 9 8 7 6 5 4 3 2 1

CONTENTS

CONTENTS

CONTENTS

INTRODUCTION

My work as an editor usually involves choosing—what to publish, how to publish it—but one of the annual joys of putting together this anthology is *not* choosing. There's an initial choice, when we (my colleagues and I at Catapult, our collaborators at PEN America) decide which three among our favorite fiction writers we'd like to ask to judge the prize. Pretty much all the hard work after that—the evaluating of submissions, the reaching of consensus—we leave to them. What a pleasure it is to be introduced this year to new writing selected by Tracy O'Neill, Nafissa Thompson-Spires, and Deb Olin Unferth.

If I see any recurring themes in these pages, they must be accidental—or it probably says more about me than it does about the judges, the original editors of the pieces, or the writers themselves. For what it's worth, this time around, I kept noticing money.

Like many people in real life, many of the characters in the stories find themselves doing things for money. In "Failure to Thrive" by Willa C. Richards, a couple of archaeologists with a newborn baby get paid to take a trip from Milwaukee to Florida to retrieve human skeletons. In vivid, painful detail, Richards describes a family nearly breaking under the pressure of competing needs: financial, physical, emotional, sexual. Money also drives people to extreme ends in Sena Moon's beguiling "Dog Dreams." The characters here are involved in an insurance scheme; as is often the case, their dire material concerns mask even more dire emotional complications.

Sometimes we talk about money when we can't talk about

feelings. In Shannon Sanders's "The Good, Good Men," two brothers meet up to confront a new boyfriend who has installed himself at their mother's house. They're convinced that the man is a penniless leech and that it's up to them to save her. Gradually, with masterful nuance, Sanders suggests that the brothers might really be there to save themselves—to protect their own memories of their childhood and their father. "Evangelina Concepcion" by Ani Cooney follows a teenage girl in the aftermath of her mother's death. She focuses on selling a box of her mother's clothes, trying to be the practical, unsentimental daughter her mother asked her to be: "You will be like steel. You can cry the first few days, but after the fifth day, I expect you to get up and help your father." The story is a bracing reminder that grief is something not everyone can afford.

The narrator of "Madam's Sister" works as a gardener and guard and odd-job man in a wealthy gated home in Zambia. Five miles away from his employer's place is the crowded township of dusty convenience shops and infested waterways where he lives. Mbozi Haimbe deftly establishes the contrasts of this world, and then inserts a visitor from London, who throws things into even starker relief. Mohit Manohar's delicately funny and suspenseful "Summertime" is about a visitor *to* London: a college student from a "newly rich" Mumbai family goes on a date with an Englishman he's met online. On its surface, their meeting promises intimacy and connection, and their city is full of refinement and luxury: an exhibit at the British Museum, high tea at the Savoy. Yet, from the beginning, there are hints that not everything is as it seems. In "Don't Go to Strangers" by Matthew Vegari, a couple lingers in another couple's home in the hours after a dinner party. They're old friends, and between them Vegari choreographs a virtuosic four-way dance of emotional shifts and unspoken tensions. In subtle ways, money—one man's work raise and fancy new barbecue grill—also creates rifts within their small social circle.

"Gauri Kalyanam" begins with a daughter being born and then quickly sold into marriage. "She is sold with the promise of cash and a cow," Kristen Sahaana Surya writes. In precise lyrical strokes, the wife is portrayed escaping her husband and working as a laborer and a housekeeper to provide for herself and her sons. She refuses her fate as "a woman whose existence depends on erasure"; money becomes her ballast, giving her substance and strength. "She sews her savings into the hems of her petticoats, and when they weigh her down, she buys thick gold belts that she fastens across her broad belly. At night her eyes close and grow green: she converts belts to houses, belts to bedrooms, belts to Western toilets and marble verandas . . . Belts trace the shape of her waist and the length of her life, and when she feels them move under her sari she feels a deep-set satisfaction."

Once I start looking, it's hard not to see this theme everywhere. In David Kelly Lawrence's "The Other Child," an unnamed narrator visits his dying father in the hospital, where he meets an unnamed child he never knew his father had. Soon the two are roaming the parks and streets of an unnamed city, meeting only strangers—but even they, in their eerie, dreamlike world, have to wait for the monthly installment of their father's inheritance before going to the market to buy fruit. In another disquieting and impressionistic story, "The Water Tower and the Turtle" by Kikuko Tsumura, a man has retired to his hometown in rural Japan because the rent is half of what he was paying in the city. His life, it seems, has also been reduced to a series of circumscribed pleasures: old memories, a bag of homemade pickles, a pack of beer, a new bike that costs just 50,000 yen. There's a new bike in "Bat Outta Hell" by Damitri Martin too, but this one is a hardly modest Harley-Davidson driven by the teenage narrator's uncle. When his mother confronts him about it—"You don't have any fuckin money! What'd you buy it with?"—the uncle replies, "None ya." This is a coming-of-age tale slyly turned inside out, where a loud motorcycle can come to represent secrecy and silence.

Valerie Hegarty's "Cats vs. Cancer" may not mention money directly; its protagonist does buy cat food and shop online for "an aesthetically appropriate cat tower" for the kitten she takes in from the alley outside her Brooklyn art studio. She also undergoes invasive diagnostic tests for breast cancer. The particularities of pet care and medical treatment are "two things you should never talk about to the person sitting next to you at a dinner party" (as the author herself says) and still the story manages to be irresistibly witty and observant and surprising. It occurs to me that money is another supposedly impolite topic of conversation, and that it's exactly this impoliteness that I keep finding and enjoying in these stories. There is a kind of candor that feels exciting, current. Like so much of the literature I love best, they show me something that's been there all along, veiled by civility and pretense and timidity and habit. They lay it bare.

I'm writing this five months into 2020, when a global crisis seems to be laying bare the profound ill health of our sociopolitical structures and economies. This might explain why money—its power, its invisibility, its tangibility, its absurdly unequal distribution, the way it forms and deforms all our relationships—has been

on my mind. Of course, it's only one facet of this multifaceted collection; other readers will find other connections and insights, will
be moved and consoled and inspired in different ways. I imagine,
however, that every last one will be left as grateful as I am to have
these twelve writers to keep us company while the world continues
to unveil itself to us. A heartfelt thanks to our judges and to the
editors of the magazines where these stories first appeared, and to
Fernanda Dau Fisher, to Jane Marchant and Clarisse Rosaz Shariyf
of PEN, and to my colleague Sarah Lyn Rogers, without whom
none of these revelations would be possible.

YUKA IGARASHI

Series Editor

BEST DEBUT SHORT STORIES 2020

EDITOR'S NOTE

"Evangelina Concepcion" paints a portrait of teenaged Lila and her small family as they weather the grief-stricken weeks after Lila's mother (the titular Evangelina Concepcion) is killed in a car accident. Told in second person, from Lila's point of view, in numbered sections and straightforward, evocative prose, the story is bleak, funny, and deeply moving.

The episodic structure of the piece effectively evokes the nonlinear, elliptical nature of Lila's grief. She writes her mother's name inside her clothes. She recalls her mother's advice: "You will be like steel." She endures visits from family friends who "praise [her] lack of frailty." She reads and rereads an online article about the accident—which offers bountiful detail about the accident's other victim, a white pedestrian, but leaves Evangelina Concepcion nameless. When a former employer of her mother's calls to express his condolences, she notices "how easy it [is] for him to cry over the phone for someone who cleaned his house." After this phone call, attempting through increasingly hysterical laughter to explain to her father, brother, and dinner guests why she found the tears of her mother's employer so funny, what Lila cannot articulate becomes as important as what does appear on the page: the outrageous emotional privilege of a man who cries freely over the death of his housekeeper is juxtaposed with Lila's own fierce stoicism in contrast so stark it becomes absurd.

That "Evangelina Concepcion" is Ani Sison Cooney's first publication is a testament to the sharp eye and editorial wisdom of our Fifteenth Anniversary Issue guest editor Alex Gilvarry. I am grateful to Alex for choosing this piece for publication, proud to work for the journal that published it, and thrilled for Ani Sison Cooney. He is truly an emerging writer to watch.

Rachel Lyon, Editor in Chief
Epiphany

EVANGELINA CONCEPCION

Ani Cooney

1.

You pulled your mother's clothes inside out and wrote *Evangelina Concepcion* with a capital *E* and a capital *C*, respectively. In black ink, you wrote behind the wide belt loops, round and round the broad belt loops, until *Concepcion*, the last name, met *Evangelina*, and they read in infinity. You wrote the name on the fat waistline and inseams until it reached the leg openings. On the back and front pockets. *Evangelina*. Behind the zipper of the fly. *Concepcion*. Then you pulled the clothes back outside in, folded them, and placed them in a large box that you labeled *Ma*.

You would find new owners for your mother's clothes. They would find movement again in a large body the size of your mother's. Wouldn't that be nice? you thought as you pushed the box in the closet. Her clothes fitted around someone else's jiggle.

Two weeks had already passed and you were coping. Your mother prepared you for a time like this, after all.

Two years ago or so, when you were only thirteen, Ma gave you orders while she was driving: "You will be like steel. You can cry the first few days, but after the fifth day, I expect you to get up and help your father." You nodded your head. "He is quite the sensitive one," she said to you. She was driving east of Wilshire Boulevard after cleaning a house in Santa Monica. You colored your fingernails black and red while you listened closely to her scenarios. In one scenario, your father was the one who died and your Ma was so debilitated that she became a child in a big woman's body. "This happens, Lila. I have seen it. I have seen women in their sixties and seventies lie and cry on the floor like they've been deboned or something. Crying like fat and slippery babies. Don't let me look like a wet baby!" she said.

You remembered that Ma gripped the steering wheel so tight her knuckles were white under thick mahogany skin. "If that ever happens, I give you the permission to throw cold water on me. Anything to wake me up, mija."

2.

Your family's accident made the news. It was quite unceremonious: the sharp T-bone occurred around eleven at night, reported in the *Los Angeles Times*, and broadcast in the early morning. You, your brother, and Ma were not named, even though you were all in the van. Your Ma reported only as the "mother of two driving the silver vehicle."

There was an online article too, and you read the condolences of strangers. One person wrote: "I know why they didn't name the mother. I bet you she doesn't have any papers." You were pissed off by this troll. You typed a response: "Your mother doesn't have papers. You asshole."

The news reported that the man who drove the BMW was going sixty miles per hour, drunk when he hit the van. A witness described the sound as a loud boom that shook the buckets of sweet beef in his Korean barbecue restaurant. Then a pedestrian was struck as the BMW zoomed into your family's car.

You slept for a long time after reading the article, and when you woke up, what you remembered most clearly was the pedestrian. Her name was Ashley Smith.

She was a volunteer football coach for underserved children in Echo Park and was heading home with a bag of oranges that night. She was a flight attendant who loved to travel and see the world. She was a good young woman, said the people who knew her well. Her favorite city was Paris.

You stared at Ashley Smith's round face and imagined that if the picture were in color, there would be pink highlights in her blond hair, just like the ones you wanted but in red and maybe dark purple. The subtle kind your mother disapproved of because your black hair set different rules. She didn't want you looking like you worked the streets of Hollywood.

You kept a copy of the newspaper article between your SAT prep books. There were a few times you reread the summary of Ashley's life, rehashing it over and over again. It was just so striking in its description that you couldn't forget Ashley's face. You really wondered what it was like to be on a plane that much and what kinds of things she did in Paris.

On a hot Friday night, over three bowls of teriyaki chicken from Panda Express, you heard your five-year-old brother, Carlos, connect the dots in a strange way. He pointed at you, at himself, and then your father.

"We're a triangle now," he whispered to you as if it were a secret.

"You don't need to whisper, Carlos," you said to him. "Say it louder." You were very firm in tone. You didn't want to baby him too much. Carlos whispered because there was a "small telephone" ringing in his ear. The doctor said that he could be suffering from mild tinnitus.

To your father, your words had quite a bite to them. Maybe it was because he had been lacking in energy the past few days and had declined construction projects up in Los Feliz, but mostly it was because you felt like you were taking care of two children. One not yet capable of understanding loss, the other impaired by the meaning of it. You heard your father say "I'm going to nap" a lot.

The night Carlos learned of your family's new shape, your father kissed him on the forehead and said good night. Then you said with real bite, "Ma did not die with pearls around her neck, you know?"

"I'll get back to work soon. Don't worry," he said. He didn't bat a sleepy eye at how cold your words were.

You did not believe him.

You let your brother watch his pastel-colored superhero cartoons for the rest of the night, his pinky finger in his right ear. He loved Sue and Johnny so much, those yellow-haired superheroes, Sue with the invisible forcefields, Johnny with the fire.

You memorized some SAT words.

You read the *LA Times* article again, never really reading the end.

You ignored your friend Katya's text messages about almost losing her virginity to that nerdy meathead who got accepted early by USC. You hoped that her mother would catch her.

It was ten thirty when Carlos walked toward you in the living room where you studied. He scratched his greasy head, put his salty fingers in his mouth, and asked, "I'm sleepy. Will Mami shower me tonight or will *you*?"

3.

The friends of your mother drove from the east, the south, and over the valley to make sure your family was well fed during this difficult time. You said thank you and embraced the mothers who delivered the carne asada on Monday, the pot of chicken and tomato soup on Wednesday, and the bowl of spaghetti with meatballs the night after even though it gave everyone in the house a bit of gas.

The mothers whispered advice to you. They told you not to be so hard on your father. He had the nervios, they added. They knew men and women in their families who took medication for this overwhelming sadness. They praised your lack of frailty. "When do you go back to school, Lila?" Josie, your mother's closest friend, asked while she washed Tupperware and covered the big bowl of spaghetti with Saran wrap.

"Late August."

"If you need help getting school materials, call me, and I'll take you with my boy," Josie said. "Just let me know." Then she proceeded to wash the dirty dishes that lay crusty near the sink.

Rosalina, one of your mother's friends and also one of the old gossips across the street, came by a few minutes later with a container of food. You hated it when she came unannounced. Your parents tolerated her because she was harmless and well into her sixties, but she annoyed you. She was always up in your business, like an auntie.

She held you close and said, "It was a beautiful funeral, Lila. Just beautiful. I attend funerals almost every year and this one is by far the nicest one I've been to. I especially liked the white doves you all released in the end." You smelled dishwashing soap on her skin, the artificial lemon kind, and you walked away.

In the kitchen, you dropped off the warm Tupperware that Rosalina brought, while she hugged your little brother and talked to your father, who sat quietly in the living room.

"She's batshit," you said to Josie. "She's always happy and smiling. There's something wrong with people like that, right?"

Josie stared at you, and she looked like she was about to tell you off, but she didn't. "I don't think so, Lila. Some people are just lucky," she said. There was no judgment in her response. "It's a perspective. Let's not be cruel."

Rosalina walked toward you and Josie in the kitchen. "Lila. Lila. Lila. Throughout this difficult time, look at what you've gained! You've gained five more mothers! Sisters! Brothers! Isn't it amazing how life works?" the old woman said. Josie looked at you and laughed a little. When everybody left, you poured the stinky black beans that Rosalina delivered down the drain.

Carlos couldn't stop sobbing that night because the ringing in his ear was loud. You shared a bedroom with him, and you told him to be quiet but he bawled anyway, his mouth open and really gummy. His breath smelled of milk and garlic.

"It's in my ear, Lila. You want to listen?"

You put your ear close to your brother's and, of course, you heard nothing. You carried him over and let him sleep next to you even though it was a warm night.

When he didn't stop crying, you pulled out a shirt from the boxes with your mother's clothes and old notebooks and perfume and you let him smell it again. It calmed him. You both fell back to sleep.

You dreamed that your mother held the bag of oranges for the children who played football in Echo Park. She carried it with one hand and walked with the cockiness of a large person down the street where Ashley Smith was struck.

In your dream, the *Los Angeles Times* wrote your mother's name instead of Ashley Smith's. Evangelina Concepcion this! Evangelina Concepcion that! She was a meticulous professional, according to her friends and employers. Your mother's favorite city, according to the article, was Los Angeles—it was the city where she learned how to drive, where you and Carlos were born, where she planned to build a modest home with a small vegetable garden. No cilantro: she wasn't fond of the smell.

You woke up from the dream with her shirt over your face. Carlos was asleep. In the summer moonlight, you saw the scribbles of name that you wrote in the clothes and that was when you decided that the box of clothes had to go.

4.

You walked past unlicensed street vendors who occupied the surrounding streets of MacArthur Park on a hot Saturday afternoon. Some men sold shiny utensils and dented woks. Some women sold blankets, children's clothes, and sundresses. Somewhere in the park, you saw an older woman hidden between two leafy trees, her bacon-wrapped hot dogs, onions, and bell peppers frying. The smoke from the grill became one with the park's permanent fountain mist. You knew why that tiny woman hid between the trees. She was considered a health and a fire hazard.

You laid out your mother's clothes on a layer of newspapers next to a man who had a pile of used shoes on the ground. You arranged the clothes by color, the names you wrote unseen. As a caveat, you placed a handwritten sign—ABSOLUTELY NO RETURNS! NO REFUNDS!—in the middle of the pile.

Two older women, one about the size and height of your mother, stopped and browsed your selection. The one who resembled your mother in height and weight looked formidable. She held up the maroon sundress your Ma loved to wear during the summer and asked, "How much is this?"

You felt guilty putting a price out loud on your mother's clothes, so you wrote the number 20 on a piece of paper and held it for the woman to see.

"It's a little expensive for a dress that no longer fits you, no? Give us a discount," the woman said while she and her friend continued to look through the clothes.

"Actually, they were my mother's."

"She must have lost a lot of weight. These clothes are big!"

"We'll have to tighten them a bit on the waist," said the other woman.

"Actually, my mother passed away."

The older women apologized to you and walked away.

The sun softened the sticky bubble gum specks on the street where you stood. It seared your skin while you smiled at people who stopped to browse and then walked along when they found the clothes an improper fit.

Someone waved at you from across the street, directly from the park's fountain. It was Rosalina.

"These clothes are still good!" she said as she stood next to you, panting from her walk. "Your mother had a lot of practical clothing."

"Nobody has bought anything yet."

"Have you been telling people they were your mother's?"

"Yes."

"And that she's passed?"

"Yes."

"Well, don't do that! The clothes of the deceased, even with any discount, are easy to resist, my dear," Rosalina said. "I've sold secondhand clothes on these streets, and buyers don't like to know that these things belonged to people who don't walk the streets anymore."

She didn't have any family that you knew of who had passed. In fact, you knew that she didn't have any family in Los Angeles at all because your Ma once told you that Rosalina had always been alone.

You thanked Rosalina. You looked at your watch and said to her, "My dad and Carlos will be home soon from the ear doctor, so I better go," and you put the clothes back in the box while Rosalina watched over you, waving at a vendor here and there.

"I'll take the bus with you," she said after you finished packing.

Rosalina was short of change, so you paid her fare. You didn't feel like leaving a sixty-year-old under the heat. You asked her whose stuff she'd sold on the streets. You wanted to know, without directly asking, who in her life had died.

Rosalina shared with you that she had a friend who worked in a Boyle Heights cemetery who gave her the unclaimed clothes of the deceased after their cremation. Rosalina received cotton baby clothes, sometimes wool with some permanent light brown stains. She received Adidas and Nike running shoes that she'd sold for quite a lot. Polo shirts, flannel shirts, jeans and dresses, blankets and hats—she acquired the clothes that the deceased had owned after their bodies were stripped, cremated, and then placed in a grave with nothing but a number over their allotted land.

Rosalina told you that she kept a silky shawl once. "It was just too nice to be sold on the streets."

She told you that the burial for the unclaimed was once a year and she took the bus all the way to Boyle Heights to stand with strangers who drove from all over the city to listen to Christian, Islamic, and Jewish prayers.

"To be honest," Rosalina whispered, "it's all very melodramatic—I think the Jewish prayer is a bit much."

She told you that an old acquaintance was buried there years ago. "We weren't lovers, but he often took me out to Denny's, which I always appreciated." Rosalina took a deep breath. The heat had exhausted her.

"That's a very sad story," you said to her.

"What was that, my dear? I couldn't hear you."

"I said that's a very sad . . ."

"Not at all! Those people are very lucky to even have a burial, you know."

You kept quiet for the rest of the ride, but Rosalina kept on babbling like she knew she'd be starved of a conversation once you both reached your destination.

5.

Your father held one of your mother's notebooks where she'd written the names and addresses of the homes she cleaned, flipping through the pages. A few sticky notes stuck out like orange tongues from the notebook. He had answered a few calls on your mother's cell phone the day before. They were from people your mother had worked for who did not know what had happened to her.

"We are so shocked and sorry to hear," they said to your father. "Let us know if there is anything we can do."

There were a couple of house owners who knew her only by a schedule, coming in at nine in the morning on a Tuesday or a Wednesday once every two or three weeks. They didn't even bother responding to your father's text messages or voice mail.

Your father didn't even ask you about the box of clothes in the living room that you tried to sell a couple of days ago.

"Thank you for your prayers, Mrs. Simpson. I am sorry I didn't tell you sooner," he said over the phone.

When he was off the phone, you told him, "Papi, please don't apologize for anything! Why do you do that?"

"I'm being courteous, Lila."

"Ma wouldn't be apologizing if it happened the other way around. We say sorry too much."

Your father looked at you, his droopy eyelids and face unsettled by what you just said to him.

The next day your friend Katya knocked unannounced at your door. Her strawberry-red hair looked choppy and oily. You didn't talk about your mother because she knew what not to ask. You allowed her to talk briefly about her USC boyfriend but told her to stop when she got into the details.

In your bedroom, you flipped through magazines and read about celebrities, their boyfriends and girlfriends and their moms and dads and the secrets that they kept.

Katya told you, "I still have some red in my place. We should dye your hair before the summer ends," and you agreed.

Your hair didn't look like the picture on the box after you

washed and dried it. Instead of amber red, your hair was the shade of a bruised and rotting beet.

"It does not look bad at all," Katya said, holding up a mirror so that you could see the back.

"Fuck you, Katya," you said, and you both sat on the bathroom floor, laughing. "My Ma was kind of right. This color makes me look like I work the streets. My hair really does set different rules," and you remembered your mother for a little bit amid the smell of ammonia in the bathroom.

Katya hugged you and you hugged her back. Before you walked home, she showed you a half-naked picture of her boyfriend, and you wished her mother would catch her.

When you got back in the apartment, you found your father cooking and Carlos in front of the TV, a piece of cotton in his right ear. Josie, her husband, Teddy, and Rosalina sat near the kitchen table with beers in hand. They said your hair looked kinda cool, but that was it. Your scalp itched and stung, but you were glad to see your father looking a little happier, a little lighter on the face while he was cooking.

Your brother said, "I like the red color." He jumped next to you on the couch. "You look just like Johnny when he's on fire in the cartoons."

The apartment smelled of greasy food, and it made you feel normal for a bit. On top of your mother's notebook, you heard your father's cell phone ring and you picked up.

It was a man named Gary. He owned a house that your mother had cleaned since Carlos was born. He was a nice older gentleman in his seventies, and you knew that he was softer than your father.

"Is this Lila? I recognize the voice," he said.

"Yes, this is Lila."

He told you that he received your father's message earlier. "I am heartbroken. Truly," he said to you. "Your mother had always been very kind to me and to my cats." You heard him begin to cry.

"It's okay, Mr. Gary. We are doing okay. Please don't cry."

"It's just very heartbreaking, that's all."

Your father asked who it was and you waved your hand at him. You walked to your bedroom to hear Gary better.

"And how is your father and your little brother?" he continued.

"They are all right, Mr. Gary."

"Golly. It breaks my heart," he continued, "I want to help. I will take care of you and your brother and your father for the rest of my life. Help as much as I can. It's the least that I can do . . ."

You almost chuckled at his offer but you didn't. You wanted to ask, "Why does it break your heart?" but instead you said goodbye and thank you to the old man.

He said that he would be in touch with your father next week. You sat at the foot of your bed and thought how easy it was for that man to offer help, how easy it was for him to cry over the phone for someone who cleaned his house.

In the kitchen, your father set up the table and everyone sat around ready to eat. Carlos was jumpy and talkative because there was company. Josie's husband had multiple construction projects coming up in the next few weeks, and he invited your father to be a part of his small team. Your father was happy to accept. He joked that he'd been sleeping for a long time. This was a good time to work, you said to your father. You were very happy for him. You sat next to Carlos and cut up the meat on his plate. You chewed your greasy food with delight.

"That was Gary on the phone," you said to everyone around the table. "He was crying like a baby . . ."

Josie looked at her husband and then at Rosalina with concern.

"I couldn't understand what else he was saying because he was crying! Like, really loudly on the phone. Like he's lost *everything*." You felt your face smiling. "He said something real funny. He said he wanted to take care of me, Carlos, and Pa for the rest of his life." You looked at your father and your visitors. Your eyes were wide. "Isn't that funny?"

You began giggling at first and then you laughed deeper, fork and spoon in your hands. You laughed while nobody else did. When you stopped for a deep breath, you looked at your father and your visitors. Rosalina and everyone else were staring at their plates.

Your father looked you straight in the eyes.

"It would be funny if you heard it. It was just the way he sounded." You turned to your side and looked at your little brother. He didn't have a clue what you found so funny.

6.

It was a week before school started, and you were ready for it all to begin again. You sat on a bus heading home with a stack of notebooks, pencils, and blank paper in a plastic bag. Your dark roots were starting to grow back, and you cut the beet-red split ends when you needed to.

The bus drove by your high school and you saw that the announcement billboard had not been updated yet. In orange pixels, the names of students who had graduated and been accepted by colleges last year entered the screen from right to left. The mothers and fathers of those students must be so proud, you thought, to see their long, bright, full names like that for all to see.

The bus drove by MacArthur Park and you saw the men and women on the streets selling used items. You were glad that you didn't have to do that for your mother's clothes again after the first time. You pressed your face against the window and watched the women walking up and down the streets, hoping you would recognize someone.

A few days after Rosalina, Josie, and her husband's visit, your father told you, "Lila, I've given away your mother's clothes and shoes." He kissed you on the forehead. "I am sorry you had to take that on. It wasn't yours to do."

He wept while looking straight at you, but you let him. There was a firmness and resolve on his face that you wanted to respect. You didn't cry with him. You just stared at how big his teardrops were.

You said to your father, "Oh. Thank you for doing that, I guess," then went to your bedroom and felt hollow, just like the first few days after the car accident. But there was also a gradual cool all over your body, a soothing after a deep sting as you sat there for a couple of hours pretending to sleep.

Your brother walked in through the bedroom door and sat by your feet.

"Are you awake?" he asked, and you opened your eyes. He told you that Rosalina dropped by earlier that day with a bowl of food, and that she was nice, that she pinched his cheeks and it hurt a little because her fingers were so rough, and that she took the box with Ma's clothes in it. "Even that shirt with the real nice smell," he said.

You stayed quiet, then asked your brother, "Did you try the food she brought? I bet she cooked it good."

You guessed that Rosalina sold or gave your mother's clothes away. Rosalina never told you. Later you kept hoping you would find someone in your neighborhood or on the bus or in the streets or in the park who wore your mother's clothes.

You stepped off the bus and walked home. Your brother greeted you at the door and invited you to play. "How about I'll be Johnny and you be Sue like the cartoons?"

You told him maybe in a little while and that you were a little tired. You kissed your father on the forehead as he sat on the couch watching the evening news.

In your bedroom, you organized your new school materials near your SAT prep books. You opened those books and found the newspaper article that reported the accident. It was funny, you remembered, how you just reread those parts about Ashley Smith, never reading the end of the article. Sorrow bent you in an odd way your Ma could never have prepared you for.

So you read again from the beginning. The facts and the report-age. The "mother of two driving the silver vehicle." The superlatives for Ashley Smith.

Then you read the end where you and your brother were mentioned. "The condition of the woman's two children was not immediately known," the report said. You read that sentence again and again and again before putting the article back in your book.

You agreed with a full heart.

You found no cruelty in those final lines.

———————

Ani Cooney is a writer based in Los Angeles. He is a graduate of UCLA, where he studied literature and creative writing. A VONA/Voices alum, he is the recipient of a Manuel G. Flores Prize from the Philippine American Writers and Artists, Inc. (PAWA). He is currently working on a collection of short stories.

EDITOR'S NOTE

David Kelly Lawrence's story came to us on our online submissions system, and neither I nor my associate editor had ever heard his name before. We both read the story and loved it immediately; I believe my associate editor said, "This is my favorite thing we've accepted since I've been working here." After I sent back the acceptance note and got David's reply, we were both amazed to learn that it was not only his first accepted story, but also the first piece of short fiction he had ever sent out. It is always fun to encounter surprises like this. If I had been asked to judge from the level of literary skill alone, I would have said this was an accomplished writer with a number of publications to his credit. Yet the story also has a freshness and originality that can perhaps be attributed in part to his newness to the field of literary endeavor. In any case, it was quite unlike anything I had read before, either in that week's batch or in the whole year of submissions.

Wendy Lesser, Editor and Publisher
The Threepenny Review

THE OTHER CHILD

David Kelly Lawrence

I HAD ALREADY finished my studies when I found out about my father's other child, the boy. I hadn't known my father was dying, or that he had another family, though to say another seems strange—I had never thought of him and my mother and me as a family, nor had I ever heard anyone call us that, though I suppose that's what we were. My father sent someone looking for me with a message to visit him at the hospital, and that's where I met the boy and his mother; we shook hands and she tried to smile and to say polite things while I watched the three of them, looking at each of their faces in turn, starting with her, then the boy, who waited quietly at her side, and lastly my father in his bed, the blanket pulled up to his chin, his eyes wide and unblinking. I remember my glasses fogging again and again, and each time I took them off to clean them on my sweater the three people in front of me lost their distinction, blurred into the wallpaper and the bedspread.

Later the woman called me, before the telephone stopped working, and she told me where she and the boy lived and when the funeral would be, though I imagine she knew I wouldn't go. I waited a few weeks and then went to her house. It was cold; leaves were whipping about and gathering in wet clumps on the curb. She came to the door almost as soon as I knocked. That day I walked with the boy around the block, we stopped to look at the papers taped to lampposts and the posters pasted on the walls. How did they get the posters to stick? he wanted to know, and I wasn't sure, so I told him they used spit, which I knew wasn't true but also didn't seem too far off. Afterwards his mother invited me in, and I said no, but I said it politely, and I thought as the door closed that she might be smiling, but really I wasn't watching her, I was watching the boy, who was already hidden in the shadow of the hallway. I came back the next week, and then after that I came every day. I would pick the boy up from school and we would go to the park, where he counted the birds that gathered around the lake as I waited silently, watching, until he grew restless and we went to ride the swings. I didn't know his age. He never cried, not that I noticed, though he did smile sometimes, towards the beginning, and then I would see that his teeth were changing, falling out and growing back.

I still read then; I hadn't stopped yet, which is fine. I am not ashamed to admit it. I am rarely embarrassed. I still had the books that my mother hadn't taken with her when she left, small detective stories made of thin yellow paper that fit nicely into the front pockets of my coat, and I would take one or two with me each day to read on the bench in the park. The books never ran out, or perhaps I just read the same ones again and again. At the end, when the killer was revealed, I almost always found that I couldn't remember the crime, or the victim—sometimes all I knew was the name of the detective, and this would make me laugh, and I would close my eyes and put my head back to see if I could feel the sun or the wind on my face.

I looked up now and again from my book to watch the boy, who would be throwing rocks at the birds or walking in slow circles around the pond. When it was cold he crouched down and tucked his hands under his legs and stared at the dirt. I had a favorite bench; we sat there every day. It was one of the older ones with fading paint, near the pond, and most of the people who sat at the benches nearby were there because those were their favorites too. I never talked to those people, though sometimes we would nod at one another, each from our own bench, though mostly everyone left each other alone. The boy didn't like the benches, and he never sat for long, perhaps because his feet couldn't touch the ground, or maybe because the restlessness that would soon set us off walking was already beginning to stir in him. Sometimes people I didn't recognize would stop and want to make small talk, and although I consider myself someone that most people like, and I am not exaggerating when I say that I put people at ease—not all people, of course, but who could say that?—I could never think of anything to say to these strangers and they would always leave soon after. I didn't like the newer benches, with their fresh green paint, or the ones by the merry-go-rounds, where the couples would sit on each other's lap and kiss. I would have liked to be in love, and I thought about it now and then. I wanted someone to think about when I finished my books and the boy was still playing, someone to occupy my mind so it wouldn't be left open to any simple thought that might come strolling along. Several times we sat on the benches by the merry-go-rounds, and the boy would count the wooden horses and I would watch the couples, but afterwards I couldn't sleep, my head ached, and we didn't go back.

When the boy's mother became sick she tried to hide it, but I could tell. I don't think the boy noticed that anything was wrong; even when she died he showed no change. He didn't want to visit her in the hospital—he would walk slower and slower as we approached, hang his head as we stood by her bed watching her sleep, the machines humming and beeping around us, and then run out the door and into the street as fast as he could when it was time to leave—and after it was all done he seemed relieved that we no longer had to visit. There was a funeral service for her as well, someone told me she would be buried near my father, but the boy and I didn't go. It was summer, there was no school, and I let him ride the swings for as long as he wanted, and when the other children lined up and complained I told their mothers that we had just come from a funeral and they left us alone. Afterwards we ate in my room, I cooked rice and sausage, and we drew with thick black markers on the wax paper that the meat came wrapped in. When it was time for bed I left the curtains open, turned out the lights, and lay awake, listening, but I didn't hear anything. Everything seemed to be the same as it had been before, even if really it wasn't, and soon we were both asleep.

When the money our father left for us arrived each month I would take the boy to the market to buy fruit and we would talk. I didn't have a very good idea about most things, but that was all right, the boy asked fewer and fewer questions, and it was clear that each day he expected less from me, from anyone. Sometimes we talked about what love might be, sitting on the low wall behind the vendors' stalls, peeling fruit, and then we would talk about adventure, and he would tell me stories he had heard or made up, stories about men in boats who got lost, men in the jungle who got lost, men in the desert who walked slower and slower until they were standing still and their bodies dissolved into puddles of sweat, or tears. He must have been taught these stories in school, or heard them from his classmates; I never saw the boy with a book, never saw him read, which was just as well. After school we still went to the park each day, even when the weather turned cold again, when the rains settled in and we were the only ones at the lake, the only ones on the swings.

When I noticed the boy growing I told him to make older friends and ask them for their old clothes, and he did, though I never saw him play with anyone else, or talk to the other children that sometimes crossed through the park. Once a week I would wash our clothes in the sink and then hang them out the window. The neighbor below had a large balcony, and our wet laundry dripped onto her table and potted plants. Once a shirt fell and landed on one of her chairs, and in the evening we heard her steps as she came up to our floor, but we didn't answer when she knocked; we both stayed where we were and watched the door. I could see the boy's breath in the coarse winter light, the pen poised in his hand. When the woman stopped knocking the boy went back to his drawing, a large maze carved out in thick black ink on the back of the sausage wrapper, which we tacked to the wall, along with the other ones, once he'd finished.

When the summer came we spent less time in the park and more time walking around the city, out around the edges where the streetlights didn't work and you could stand under the highways and touch the pillars that held up the cars and feel them vibrate. At first the boy would grow tired, and after five or six hours of walking I would have to carry him on my back. With time, though, he became stronger, and when the leaves began to turn colors he could go until sundown without stopping, and I was the one who would become thirsty and begin to flag, though I would like to think I didn't show it. Everyone we passed was a stranger; I never noticed the same face twice. School had begun, but the boy didn't go back, and neither of us mentioned it. We talked instead about the concrete, which stretched farther than we could see, about the buildings that made up our horizon, and he described everything we looked at as we walked: the boarded-up stores that we passed, the cars that sat empty in rows and the ones that dragged themselves down the middle of the street, the difference between the color of the sidewalk—where it existed—and the road. I told him that the pillars holding up the highway were full of bones, that they had been filled by the president himself, but the boy didn't ask who the president was, or whose bones they were, he just nodded and kept walking.

Some nights we returned late, and I would sleep a deep and dreamless sleep while the boy sat on the floor and drew. Other nights he would continue walking and I would come back to the room alone, waking in the morning to find him seated in the chair, watching the reflection of the sunrise in the windows of the building across the courtyard. When people began to appear in those windows he would turn away, wait for me as I dressed, then put on his shoes, and we would leave. I asked him once where he slept on those nights, but he shook his head, and finally after a long silence he said—not turning around, a few steps ahead of me—that he slept as he walked, he crossed the city in his sleep. Like a man who navigates the rooms of his home in the dark, without reaching for the light, he said, and though I knew that the boy's answer should unnerve me, that my skin should rise and shiver, the truth is I felt at ease, I was relieved, and I took a breath and asked him if he dreamt while he walked, too, but he was silent, and though I could only see the back of his head I knew that his eyes were shut, that he was awake but his eyes were closed tight as if he were sleeping, and I knew also, though he didn't make a sound, that he was laughing.

Each day we walked farther than the day before, and one evening we came upon a cemetery. We passed beneath the gate and found a sprawl of slouching concrete tombs lined up along cobblestone paths. I watched the snow being tossed about by the wind, gone before it reached the ground. The boy disappeared among the headstones, and I followed slowly after, beginning at the edge, beneath a wall of trees cut short at stunted angles, then into the center, where the paths were unruly and long. Some graves were new and ornate, decorated with pictures and flowers, but most were old and bare, some fading, some broken open, others sinking into the dirt they marked. At the end of one row I found two headstones side by side, decorated with small tiles that shone bright despite the clouds hanging above. The snow was beginning to stick, wet shivers clinging to the tops of the graves. Beneath the tiles were names, carved deep in the stone, followed by numbers. I read the words, and then I read them a second time, and I closed my eyes and saw the snow dancing against the dark wall of my eyelids. I couldn't remember the names, they were already gone, and when I looked again they disappeared in front of me, each letter melting away as my eyes moved to the next, and so I shut them tight, took off my glasses, tried to remember my father's name and the name of the woman who had shaken my hand when I met the boy, tried to remember their faces, but I couldn't, there was nothing, only the snow. I called out for the boy and was met with silence, and then I called again and my voice disappeared with the wind and the snow.

That night I slept alone, and when I woke the chair by the window was empty. I walked to the park and found my bench, and in the evening when I returned to the room I cooked rice and sausage, and I flattened the wax paper and left it on the counter by the sink. In the morning I walked back to the park and I counted the birds around the lake; a stranger nodded at me and I closed my eyes, and when it grew dark again I returned to the room and found the door locked. I could hear soft noises inside, bare feet moving back and forth across the floor. I knocked, and waited, and then I knocked again; I heard water run and oil pouring into a hot pan, and then a hush fell over the room, over the hallway, a heavy quiet that pulled at my eyelids and settled into the snow melting in my hair and on my coat, until it was broken by the sound of my footsteps as my feet carried me down the hall to the stairs, out the door, into the night where the snow was still falling, batted about by the wind, captured for a moment beneath the streetlights and then disappearing into the night.

———————

David Kelly Lawrence lives in Vincennes, France, and is studying for a master's degree in library science.

EDITOR'S NOTE

Published in *Michigan Quarterly Review*'s special issue on contemporary Europe, Mohit Manohar's "Summertime" takes place in London, on the eve of the 2016 Brexit vote. Sandeep, a college student who grew up in Mumbai, goes on a first date with Russ. In his online search for romance, Sandeep encounters plenty of (badly punctuated) "casual racism": to wit, "no asians no blacks—not racist just a preference." Russ's claim that he's "into racially diverse men" appeals to the lonely Sandeep, who fantasizes about a potential soulmate while studying at the library. The pair stroll through an exhibit at the British Museum, kiss beside a courtyard fountain, enjoy high tea at the Savoy Hotel. Manohar's rich description and leisurely pacing keenly lay the way for the disillusionment to come.

With its sensitive yet unsentimental portrayal of a young man abroad, "Summertime" offers an intimate coming-of-age story. It also delicately but forcefully resonates with cultural and political implications. Over petits fours and rosé, the impending Brexit vote comes up in conversation. "We'll definitely remain," Russ says, and Sandeep responds, "I haven't yet met a single person who thinks differently." "Precisely," Russ concludes. Manohar precisely subverts expectations and elegantly delivers harsh news. Great deployment of an umbrella "with a tip that looked primed to impale people," too.

Polly Rosenwaike, Fiction Editor
Michigan Quarterly Review

SUMMERTIME

Mohit Manohar

IN HIS JUNIOR year at Yale, Sandeep slept with a boy for the first time, and this filled him with such guilt that he knew he had to tell his mother. His parents had recently moved to an even taller apartment building in Mumbai: its topmost floors had a view of both the Arabian Sea and the Bombay Harbour. Only ten years ago, they had lived like regular people in the northern part of the city. But then his father's New Age Ayurveda business took off, and when it became too big for him to manage alone, he sold it to a larger wellness company, whose stockholders elected him to its board of directors. Suddenly they had a lot of money. Sandeep was plucked from his regular school and put in an institution where the children of the rich went. There he acquired excellent English and French and lost his ability to speak good Hindi. He and his parents learned to use *vacation* as a verb; they vacationed abroad. They stayed in expensive hotels in London and Paris, where they suffered embarrassments big and small because they were still, essentially, middle class. When his parents felt insulted, his mother wished that their lives were simpler, that they still lived in their old neighborhood. His father merely looked like a chided child, absorbing a new lesson in propriety. During these moments, Sandeep felt embarrassed by his mother's melodrama and annoyed by his father's meekness.

They struggled to keep pace with their changing lives. They were not bad people. He wanted to protect them.

"Ma, I have something to say." When he Skyped with her, it was evening in New Haven, the sun only rising in Mumbai. He told her, in overwrought phrases, that he thought of boys instead of girls.

She said, "You know, Sandeep, there are good things in life, and there are bad things in life, and often it is hard to tell which is which."

"Ma, what are you saying? Do you understand what I am saying?"

"I understand perfectly well."

They stared at each other in silence, half the world between them. The Skype connection was surprisingly good.

"Promise me one thing," his mother said. "You will reconsider this decision of yours."

"This is not a decision of mine."

"Then promise me something else," she said. "You will not do anything to embarrass us."

SANDEEP WAS SPENDING a month in London that summer. He had won a senior thesis research grant and planned on looking at John Lockwood Kipling's archives at the British Library. When he got to London and bothered to compute costs, he realized that he could last the month if he didn't eat anything and walked everywhere. His mother told him to use the credit card she had given him.

"So you can track what I'm doing?" he asked over Skype.

"At least I'll know you're eating."

He spent his mornings and afternoons at the British Library and imagined that one day, the pretty boy across the table would ask,

"What are those sketches you're looking at?" And he would tell him that these were made by Rudyard Kipling's father, who was an artist in his own right. They would start a conversation and the boy would ask if he wanted to get coffee when the library closed. And even though he didn't drink coffee, he would go.

Or he would be waiting in the queue to return a book on Kipling, and a bespectacled man in a sports jacket standing behind him would comment on Kipling's lasting artistic influence on the Indian subcontinent, which would spark a conversation between them, and this man would ask, around closing time, if he wanted to get a beer. And even though he didn't like beer, he would agree.

But his time in the library remained solitary and he struggled to understand how one went about doing archival research. Kipling's papers bored him. The note-taking was tedious. No boy or man noticed him.

Online, London was full of attractive men, all into "dates and mates," but whose profiles warned: "dont message me if youre less than 6'," "dont message me if youre less than 8"," "no asians no blacks—not racist just a preference," "if I dont reply Im not interested." When he came across a profile of a doctor—twenty-eight years old, five foot eleven, pronounced jawline, well-kept stubble—who was "into racially diverse men," he thought, what could be the harm in messaging him? He drafted something clever but it sounded desperate. Eventually, he sent, "Hey, how're you?" The beauty of his query, he thought, lay in its use of punctuation. But the man did not reply. He came online and he went offline. Sandeep felt lonely and depressed. Even a psychopathic man (what other kind of person would write on his dating profile that he likes "racially diverse men"?) was not interested in him. He edited his bio—"from Mumbai, study at Yale, pic taken from last vacation in Tokyo, in

London for the month"—and then felt pathetic for showing off in this manner. He deleted the app.

THERE WERE OTHER students from Yale, mostly Americans, who were spending their summer in London. They met up occasionally for drinks in pubs, thrilled that they didn't need fake IDs to gather there. The conversations always returned to the same theme: how different England was from America.

"I mean, in most countries people drive on the right side," said Peter, a peevish blond guy that all the girls admired. "Studies show this is safer. I could not drive on the wrong side."

"It isn't that difficult," Sandeep said, "I drive both in India and the States." He had said this to impress Peter but received a dismissive look instead.

They were sitting in a poorly lit and dank pub not far from his Airbnb. Each pub they'd been to had a similar aura of darkness and mystery. Sandeep felt he had gone back in time, to Tudor England perhaps, and that outside, he would stumble upon a beheading or a bonfire raised to burn a witch. The summer light stretched long into the evening, but night eventually arrived. When Peter left, many girls departed. When another pretty brunette left, the few boys followed her out. He was left nursing his second glass of wine in the company of Kat, a sleek girl from New York who always wore black, and who was on her fourth gin and tonic.

"Gin in London is really good," she said in her husky voice. After a pause, she added, "I went on a date with someone yesterday."

"That's exciting," said Sandeep. "How did you meet him?"

"I met her," Kat said. "I met her online." Then she looked at him intently, her eyes shining in the dim pub light. "I see the way you look at Peter," she whispered, and took a sip of her gin and tonic.

Sandeep realized he was perspiring. The wine and the summer and his inability to hide were making him warm. He paid for his drinks, Kat paid for hers, and then he walked her to the Camden Town Underground. Back at his Airbnb, he downloaded the app he had deleted two days ago. The psychopathic doctor interested in racially diverse men had written back: "Hey sorry for the late response. Was busy with work. Hows London treating you. Im Russ whats your name."

THEY CHATTED ON the dating app and then exchanged numbers and took the conversation to WhatsApp. Sandeep still had his American number, which gave him unlimited 2G but charged dearly for international calls and texts. But only old people texted or called.

Russ suggested they meet at the British Museum on Sunday, when he didn't have to report for work. On Sunday morning, Sandeep put on a T-shirt and a pair of jeans, appraised himself in the mirror, and thought, no, too casual. He changed into a white linen shirt and blue trousers. This looked appropriate and summery. He reached the British Museum at the appointed hour, ascended the marble stairs, and waited.

A man tapped him on his right shoulder from behind. He turned.

"You're Sandeep, right? I'm Russ." He was smiling and Sandeep straightaway noticed that he did not have crooked teeth and that he had also made some effort to impress, dressed, as he was, in a crisp shirt, khakis, and oxfords. Either his brown hair was graying or he had chosen a peculiar highlight.

"Did I say that right? Sand-eep?"

"Actually, it is Sun-deep. Shall we go inside?"

Russ carried a large black umbrella, with a tip that looked primed to impale people. It was sunny out. "Umbrella," Sandeep said, like a child recognizing an object and saying its name.

"Yes, you can never trust London's weather," Russ replied.

They were there to see the special exhibition *Sunken Cities: Egypt's Lost Worlds*. The galleries were blue-green and cool, and on a large wall a video of a sunken city was projected. Fish swam among placid Egyptian statues green with algae, and underwater archaeologists floated towards these statues and touched them in amazement with gloved hands. The wall text read:

Vanished beneath the waters of the Mediterranean, the lost cities of Thonis-Heracleion and Canopus lay at the mouth of the Nile. Named after the Greek hero Heracles, Thonis-Heracleion was one of Egypt's most important commercial centres for trade with the Mediterranean world and, with Canopus, was a major centre for the worship of the Egyptian gods. Their amazing discovery is transforming our understanding of the deep connections between the great ancient civilisations of Egypt and Greece.

Speakers hidden in the galleries played the sound of waves breaking upon a shore, and on the ceiling was projected a video of water: rippling, glittering, shining like a jewel. Sandeep glanced at one object and then the next, while Russ took his time, mesmerized by each gold coin that had been extracted from the sea. Sandeep walked out of the first room and then realized that Russ was still behind. He retraced his steps and found Russ studying a lopsided glass ewer with a thread of gold running around its lip and base.

"Amazing, isn't it, that this vessel lay in what it was meant to carry for thousands of years?" Russ said.

For something to lie in what it was meant to carry: that was a nice way to put it.

Sandeep adjusted his pace to Russ's, and they exchanged comments on the strange things they saw, but as they progressed through the show, they became quieter, communicating with eye gestures and smiles. To Sandeep it felt like an intimate language. Occasionally Russ took it upon himself to explain things. He shared the little he knew about hieroglyphs and talked about the one time he had gone underwater diving ("sadly not near a sunken city"). Sandeep listened and nodded, enjoying the singsong cadence of his accent. He liked the way light reflected against Russ's blue eyes, made brighter by the blue of the ceiling, how they occasionally caught a glint of the gold from the cases.

When they emerged from the gallery, Sandeep blinked. He had forgotten where he was, and some part of him did feel he was underwater, for the world outside had transformed as well. The glass ceiling in the museum atrium, through which only an hour ago the summer sun streamed, now showed an inky sky above.

"See," said Russ, lightly tapping his umbrella to the floor. "Aren't you glad I have this? Let's walk outside. London is beautiful in the rain."

They walked close to each other under the umbrella, heading south towards Covent Garden. A few street entertainers were performing their magic tricks in the piazza, the rain unable to deter them. Some tourists, sheltered underneath umbrellas and raincoats, watched and took videos on their phones.

They spoke about their pasts. Russ was Scottish, born not far from Edinburgh, where he attended college. Then he relocated to Australia for work but got bored with that country. "People there love to spend all of their time outdoors. I liked the outdoors, but there are no museums there. Hardly any culture." He lived in France next, but not before he got the chance to go to India. "I was in Goa, mostly. Those were the days I was a serious alcoholic. No, really. I may not look like one, but I had a real drinking problem. It was New Year's Eve, I remember, and a bunch of us were sitting around the table, talking, drinking, and I got up to use the loo and just collapsed. When I woke up, sick and tired, I said to myself, no more. And I haven't touched a drop since."

They walked to the courtyard of the Courtauld and sat on the metal chairs near the fountain. The rain was beginning to peter out and the sun hesitatingly shone again. Students and tourists walked in and out of the damp neoclassical buildings, and children ran through the jets of the fountain, squealing with joy. One chubby boy gave Sandeep a long and curious look, a finger in his nose, the other hand scratching his bum. Then he ran through the fountain, shrieking with delight as water hit him from below, into the hands of his mother.

Sandeep told Russ about his childhood in the northern part of Mumbai. By 5:50 a.m. each day, he had to be out of his house in the noisy apartment complex, the bus stand a ten-minute walk away. There was always a scuffle to get into the bus. The ones who got in early were able to find a seat, while the rest of them had to stand. He often had to stand. Sometimes, the senior boys would ask him if he wanted to take turns sitting on their laps.

He loved his family's weekend trips to south Mumbai. They would take the local train from the Borivali station near their house: the train speeding through the colorful, blurry city; the thrill of the wind hitting his face. They would step out on the platform of Victoria Terminus, which would always be crowded, and his mother would offer him her hand. "Look ahead, not above," she would admonish when he looked up, mesmerized by the station's Gothic ceiling. He described it to Russ: the white vaults with blue dots and ribs outlined in gold.

"Have you seen the ones at St. Pancras, inside the hotel area?" asked Russ. "They also have golden ribs, but the vaults are green, if I remember correctly."

"St. Pancras actually provided the inspiration for Victoria Terminus," said Sandeep. "A portion of my senior thesis looks at this connection. But I don't want to bore you with talk of my thesis."

"It's not boring at all. Do you have a picture of this station?"

"Not on my phone, but I'm sure Google will have something."

Sandeep pulled out his phone and googled "Victoria Terminus ceiling." Russ pulled his chair closer to look at the phone, and the length of Sandeep's left arm pressed against the length of Russ's right. He turned to face him and found, quite unexpectedly, his tongue inside Russ's mouth, which tasted a little like peppermint and—was it orange candy?—yes, like the orange candy he used to have as a boy. Russ's eyes were closed; he closed his eyes as well. He could hear the kids playing in the fountain, but the sound seemed distant and quaint, as though they were in a countryside by the river.

"Well, that was nice," Russ said when they pulled apart. "So, let's see this lovely station of yours."

The chubby boy was back again, staring intently.

"Ignore him," his mother shouted from across the fountain. "He's just curious."

They both laughed and Russ made a jerking motion, as if to catch the boy. This led the child to emit a delighted shriek and he sprinted across the fountain, again into the hands of his mother.

"You have a good day," Russ called to her.

To Sandeep he asked, "What do you want to do next?"

"Anything you'd like. I'm open."

"Well, since you don't drink coffee, and I don't drink alcohol, do you want to go to the Savoy nearby for afternoon tea? It's really good, if you haven't tried it yet."

"I'd love to. But I don't think I should spend that much money."

"Says the person who studies at Yale and vacations in Tokyo," said Russ mockingly.

"Hey, don't make fun. I had to say something to catch people's attention. You've no idea how much casual racism there is on these sites. But no, I shouldn't spend that much money."

"I completely understand," said Russ. "How about this: you pay what you're comfortable paying and I'll cover the rest."

"Are you sure?"

"Yes, of course, why would I offer otherwise? I do make a doctor's salary, you know, and today is such a lovely day. And you are such lovely company."

In spite of himself, Sandeep blushed. "But are we dressed properly to go to the Savoy?" he asked.

Russ leaned back and looked Sandeep up and down. "You look marvelous."

The hotel was a five-minute walk away. Its large marquee, crowned by the statue of a sentry, tempted passersby with promises of opulence, and when one walked into the foyer, a world of luxury opened before the eyes, in which broad-shouldered men in fine tailored suiting and shapely women in elegant dresses leaned gently towards each other, while servers glided around and were at one's side to carry out wishes one hadn't even articulated.

"Welcome to the Savoy," a hostess greeted them. "How may I help you?"

"We've come here for your afternoon tea," said Russ.

"Very well, gentlemen. Do you have a reservation?"

"I'm afraid not, but I was wondering if you'd be able to accommodate us."

"Give me a moment, please," she said, and departed to check with a colleague. True to her word, she returned in a moment. "Please follow me, gentlemen," she said, smiling a professional, wrinkle-free smile.

They walked into a large room with a stained-glass cupola at its center, glowing in the sun. Below the cupola was an indoor gazebo, and underneath this was a pianist playing on a Steinway. Brocaded and upholstered armchairs and regal wooden tables covered with silk tablecloths were arranged around the gazebo. They were led to a table for two.

"Have you gentlemen dined with us before?"

"I have, but my friend hasn't," said Russ.

"Welcome back, sir," she said to Russ, seating him, and to Sandeep, "I do hope you enjoy our service, sir."

"I already am, this place is beautiful," said Sandeep, a little too earnestly.

The hostess smiled even harder—it must hurt to smile so much—and said, "Your server will be with you shortly."

"Welcome to the Savoy, gentlemen." A man in sharp business

attire came up to their table, carrying leather-bound books, which were actually their menus. "I'm David, and I'll be taking care of you this afternoon."

"Thank you, David," said Russ. "We're simply here for your high tea."

"Perfect. Would you like the Traditional Afternoon Tea or the Traditional High Tea?"

"Do you want a minute to decide?" asked Russ.

"What did you have the last time you were here?" asked Sandeep.

"The Traditional High Tea, I believe."

"And what're you getting now?"

"The Traditional High Tea, I believe." Russ smiled.

Sandeep couldn't help smiling back. "Two Traditional High Teas it is, then," said Sandeep, addressing David.

"Very well, sirs, which kind of tea would you like?"

"I'll go with Ceylon," said Russ.

"And I'll have Darjeeling," said Sandeep.

The server collected the menus and began to walk away. "Actually, David," said Russ. David turned around and nearly hopped back to their table. "Would you mind adding the Deutz Rosé to our order?" Sandeep raised his eyebrows, and Russ said, "Don't worry, it's on me."

"Would that be by the glass or by the bottle, sir?"

"I think the bottle will do."

When the server left, Sandeep said, "I thought you didn't drink."

"I don't. But today feels like a special day, and I thought, why not?"

"You really shouldn't be paying so much money on my behalf," said Sandeep.

Russ took Sandeep's hands. "Sorry, I didn't mean to offend," he said. "I thought you were okay with me paying. We can cancel the bottle."

"No, it's fine." Sandeep felt stupid for having protested. Here was someone who was noticing him, not just noticing but being kind and generous to him. "I'm just—well, thank you."

"The pleasure is all mine."

Sandeep turned towards the Steinway. "Do you know this piece?"

The melody floated above the murmur of voices and the gentle clanging of silverware on ceramic. "I'm afraid I don't," Russ said.

"It sounds like Chopin to me," said Sandeep. "There used to be a jewelry ad in India that had this music. I find it so beautiful. And sad."

"Why sad?"

"Well, doesn't it sound a little sad to you? Listen."

They listened together. The music leapt from a note promising a happy progress, but, inexplicably, it stumbled upon one minor key and then another, each filled with longing, and all this revealed only the naïveté of that earlier impression. Russ didn't say anything but looked at Sandeep in a way to say he understood what he meant. Finally, someone who did.

David returned with an afternoon tea stand carrying little finger sandwiches and scones so yellow they looked like dollops of butter. Alongside these were white clotted cream and blood-red strawberry preserve. The tea service was all in silver. Another server approached them with a large tray, on which were placed an assortment of petits fours—chocolate éclairs, strawberry macarons, lemon tarts, vanilla cannelés—and, as though this wasn't enough, an additional server approached them with a trolley table, which carried a selection of cake slices—gateau, pavlova, cheesecake, carrot cake. They ate and talked and the hour passed by. When they could eat no more, the bottle of Deutz Rosé came. The sommelier poured a sip for Russ, who pronounced it excellent. They were offered two glasses of rosé and they leaned back in the comfort of their armchairs.

Sandeep was glad Russ had suggested the hotel and the rosé. He wanted to thank him, but saying "thank you" would seem so formal now.

"The Brexit vote count is tonight," Russ was saying.

"And?"

"And we'll definitely remain."

"I haven't yet met a single person who thinks differently."

"Precisely."

The rosé was making Sandeep a little sleepy. On the one hand, he wanted this luxurious experience to never end. On the other hand, he wanted Russ to take him home and fuck him out of his mind. He thought of his last and only date: they had watched a Meryl Streep movie on the laptop in his room while nibbling on cheese and crackers, left over from some college event.

"What are you thinking of, Mister?" Russ asked.

"I am thinking—" Sandeep almost blurted out what he was thinking. "I'm thinking that I've never had a first date this good."

"Let's drink to that," said Russ, holding up his wineglass.

Russ was telling Sandeep about the time the Brexit bus nearly hit him—"that would have been a fun lawsuit"—when he felt his pocket. "Who's calling me?" he muttered, pulling his phone out. "They're not supposed to call me on Sunday. Hello, yes, who's this?" He mouthed "Hospital" in Sandeep's direction.

Sandeep nodded.

"Yes, yes," said Russ on the phone. "What does the cardio

report say?" He got up from his chair, mouthed "One minute" to Sandeep, and stepped out of the room.

Sandeep's eyes followed him. He hoped the call wouldn't be long, and he hoped that Russ was not being summoned to the hospital. He was hoping to spend the evening and the rest of the night with him. Surely the rosé would help, and it wouldn't hurt as much as the last time. He just had to relax and all would be fine. He looked at the armchair where Russ had been sitting and saw his large umbrella lying on the floor. He picked it up, examined it, and then put it back on the floor, lest Russ suddenly return and catch him admiring it. Although, why shouldn't he be admiring it? It was a handsome umbrella.

And when Russ returned, they would pay the bill, and Sandeep would say something to indicate that he was open to going to Russ's place. His own Airbnb had a shabby feeling about it. Besides, he didn't have any lube. Russ looked like a man who would be prepared for such occasions. He would tell him to go slow at first. Russ wouldn't mind, he hoped.

But what if he did? Relax, Sandeep told himself, and drank the last of the rosé. He looked at the umbrella and was strangely aroused by it. Should he get the check so they could speed things up? Where was Russ? When five minutes passed and Russ did not return, Sandeep decided to WhatsApp him. He opened the app on his phone and saw that Russ was no longer on his list of contacts.

Surely his WhatsApp was acting up. He went on the dating app where they had started chatting and saw that Russ's profile had disappeared from there as well. He could feel his heart beating faster. He got up from his armchair and asked a server to point him in the direction of the men's room. The men's room had large spotless mirrors and a calming aroma that had no effect on Sandeep. Russ wasn't in any of the stalls. Nor was he in the lobby.

Sandeep returned to the table, and David, sensing perhaps that something was amiss, brought the check. Sandeep looked at the amount and tried to hide his shock. He put down the credit card linked to his mother's bank account.

"My friend had to leave," he blurted. "He's a doctor. He got a call from the hospital."

David merely nodded in reply. He returned with a receipt that Sandeep signed. The image of his mother, sitting at the dining table at home and going through the credit card bill, flashed in front of his eyes. He brushed it aside.

"Would you like a copy of your receipt, sir?"

What was the point? "Yes, sure."

Sandeep walked to the lobby and then through the revolving door and found himself expelled from paradise onto the busy sidewalk of the Strand. While he was still wondering what to do, a young man from the hotel came running to him.

"Sir," he said. For a second, Sandeep thought that Russ had been found inside the hotel in a delirious state, or dead, and that this was all a grave mistake. But the man only said, "You left your umbrella."

Sandeep looked at the large black umbrella with its sharp tip and overcame the urge to impale the messenger with it. He took the umbrella and said thanks.

He began walking, not knowing where he was going. He was furious. He felt humiliated. Why would anyone go to such lengths to fool somebody? Or was there genuine misunderstanding and Russ had hated something about him so strongly that he'd simply walked out? Then he remembered he still had Russ's number. So what if it costs a fortune to call? He had already paid a fortune.

He dialed the number; his call wouldn't go through. He opened Skype on his phone and called from there. The 2G was awfully slow. The phone finally rang but no one picked up. He tried again. No response.

He wanted to smash his phone on the pavement. How could he not have seen this? How was he so stupid? So many things Russ had said or done should have alerted him: when he ordered the bottle of rosé, for instance; or when he suggested they go to the Savoy; or even the fact that Russ had replied to his message only after he had updated his bio with information designed to impress. Russ's bio in itself should have warned him, but instead he had thought that here was a white guy trying to prove he wasn't racist and not knowing how to do it. He wanted to shout, and in fact, he did, to the alarm of those walking near him on the sidewalk.

THE NEXT MORNING, he woke up to a call from his mother. He was still working out what to say to her.

"Did you see the news?" she asked.

Maybe she hadn't checked her online banking. "What news?"

"You're at the place where history is in the making!"

He opened his laptop. His social media had exploded. He skimmed through a *Guardian* article a friend had posted on Facebook. And he felt . . . he felt strangely happy. Good, he thought. This is exactly what should happen. Take that, Russ. Or whatever your actual name is.

"Maybe now they'll give the Kohinoor back," his mother said.

"I initially felt bad. And then I thought—my god, why am I feeling bad for the British?"

They were laughing.

"Also, my bank sent me an alert yesterday, but I only saw it this morning. Can you check that you didn't misplace the credit card? I see this huge charge from the Savoy. I'm guessing it wasn't you."

The Savoy had a receipt with his signature on it. "Ma," he said. "It was me. Let me explain."

Mohit Manohar was born and raised in India and is currently a graduate student in the History of Art Department at Yale University. His fiction has received a Ward Prize and a Francis LeMoyne Page Creative Writing Award from Princeton University. He is working on his dissertation on medieval India and a novel set in contemporary India.

EDITORS' NOTE

When this story first showed up in our queue, we knew it wasn't quite ready for publication and yet we just couldn't let it go. There was something raw and alive about it, and the voice held such intimacy, anguish, and—the real surprise—humor. It also covered some unpromising-seeming subject matter that turned out to be rich with metaphor and subtle beauty: torturous medical procedures, feral cats, and urban snow. After hanging on to the story for a while, unsure what to do, we took a chance and asked the author if she'd be willing to revise. When she sent the story back nearly three thousand words shorter but missing none of its original charm, we realized that this first-time writer knew what she was doing all along. Our response to the revision was a definitive and jubilant *yes!*

We later learned that Valerie Hegarty is an accomplished painter and sculptor. She's also been filling notebooks with writing for her whole life. She's wanted to be a writer since fourth grade, she says, but never sent her work out until now. She took a risk by submitting this very personal story, and as editors we were gratified by her trust, her artistry, and her hard work.

There was always something improbable about this publication. Not just because it was by an unpublished author and first came in at an unwieldy ten-thousand-plus words, but as Valerie herself has said, "My story is about two things you should never talk about to the person sitting next to you at a dinner party—that you have cancer and two cats!" And yet here it is, not only beloved by its editors at the *New England Review*, but also proudly situated among the PEN/Dau Short Story Prize's dozen debuts.

Carolyn Kuebler, Editor
Ernest McLeod, Fiction Editor
New England Review

CATS VS. CANCER

Valerie Hegarty

I THROW THE bandage in the trash can with the clumped kitty litter. I ask the kitty lying with me on the bed on top of the covers, "Did you do your best today? Did you show up and do what you needed to do today?"

The kitty rolls lazily onto her back and stretches out her arms and legs like she's in rigor mortis. She was recently neutered and I rub her shaved belly and mending incision line. She is purring. She is black with long white feet and white front paws, a white chin and half a white nose.

"Kitten mittens!" I say, rubbing her belly. "Cat jammies! You did a great job today, kitty!"

I adjust the ice pack under my bra. When I lifted my bra up in front of the mirror earlier, there was blood on the outer surgical bandage. I remember the nurses said if I see some blood, that's normal.

THE FIRST TIME I saw the kitten was a month earlier, after I started renting an art studio on the basement floor of a warehouse building in the far reaches of Brooklyn. I worked on a painting for a few hours and then took a break to look out the window. The basement studio window was eye level with an alley. Looking back at me on the other side of the glass was a little black kitten. I looked away, dismayed. When I looked back, hoping she'd be gone, there were two little black kittens looking at me. I looked away again uneasily and when I looked back there were three little kittens—two black ones and a black one with a white nose and white paws. Again I looked away, this time on the verge of panic, and when I looked back there were four little kittens looking back at me through the window—two black ones and two black ones with white noses and paws. I turned away, went on my computer, and googled "What to do when you can't save the world." I read several posts, turned out the light, and left for the day.

The next day there were no kittens in the morning but by afternoon one of the little black ones appeared at the window, and over the course of an hour she multiplied into four. They batted at broken glass and chased the plastic lids of coffee cups to and fro in front of the window. They scratched around in abandoned planters and bit each other's necks. They would stop occasionally to stare in the window.

I went and bought a bag of cat food at the deli. At dusk they lined up on the broken sidewalk and watched me with eight green eyes as I filled chipped bowls with cat food. Their white whiskers twitched in unison and they moved their heads like they were watching a tennis game as I swept up the broken glass in their garbage-can-alley home.

A large gray cat seemed to watch over the kittens. Sometimes when I walked from the subway to the art studio the large gray cat would emerge from an alley several blocks away and walk ahead of me on the sidewalk. We would both turn right, then turn left, then I would open the gate while the large gray alley cat scooted underneath, both of us ending up at the bowls to feed and watch the kittens.

At night I went on the internet and read about the difference between stray and feral cats, the cat overpopulation epidemic in New York City, and the mayor's new campaign to handle the epidemic with TNR (trap-neuter-return). A concerned citizen is advised to contact a rescue organization, then take a class to learn how to trap the animal and bring it to the ASPCA for neutering. Then the neutered cat is to be returned to its original location to live out its life on the streets. I realized the large gray alley cat's clipped ear was not a dogfight injury but a universal sign that he had been trapped-neutered-returned.

There were inquiring phone calls, sad kitty posters, desperate pleas to neighbors, and sleepless nights worrying about the kittens. After a month, my sad kitty posters attracted two other codependent caregivers. We joined forces to get the kitties TNR'd, but then in the end we didn't have the hearts to release them back to the alley. We quickly got three of the four kittens adopted. After much cajoling from the other ladies—"Two cats are better than one! I have four cats already or I'd take one! How can you not love a kitten? Your older cat will love a little friend!"—I begrudgingly took home the most fearless tuxedo.

"Say goodbye to your sisters," I told the feral kitten as I cornered her and pushed her into the carrier. "You are never going to have to play with broken glass again."

The kitten's first day at my apartment was a nightmare. When I released the kitty to her new home, she promptly scrambled into my closet and disappeared. My older cat rushed in like a rabid raccoon, straight into the back of the closet, and a ferocious attack ensued. I grabbed the older cat and she turned on me, biting my hand hard. I held tight and tossed her out of the bedroom and shut the door, adrenaline surging. My hand was bleeding. The new kitty was squeezed into the farthest back corner of the closet. Was this safer than releasing the kitten back in the alley? I wasn't so sure anymore.

The next day, I had a mammogram and ultrasound scheduled, due to a small lump in my left breast. I wasn't worried. This had happened before. All previous diagnostic tests had revealed benign cysts. I called my friend who had two cats and fibrocystic breasts. We agreed the diagnostic tests were annoying but necessary, and my friend recommended reading a book called *Cat vs. Cat* to ensure a better outcome from my new cat introduction.

I downloaded *Cat vs. Cat* on my Kindle so no one would see what I was reading in public. There was a two-hour delay for diagnostic mammograms and ultrasounds, and I welcomed the opportunity to be educated in cat behavior while sitting in the series of waiting rooms. In the outer waiting room we got to keep our clothes on, and an occasional husband, son, or fiancé sat with a woman, but no men were allowed in the inner waiting room. We were all given lockers and instructed to remove everything from the waist up. In the inner waiting room we were reduced to our pants, winter boots, and flimsy wraparound gowns. The women who must have done this multiple times this winter were smart enough to wear button-down sweaters that they kept outside their lockers and draped on their shoulders.

Most women were looking at their cell phones instead of the pile of women-themed magazines: *Redbook*, *Glamour*, *People*, *Self*. There was a lone *Sports Illustrated*, presumably left behind by a stray male companion. We all had our locker keys attached to colored plastic slinkies around our wrists. I settled into *Cat vs. Cat*, tilting the screen when an embarrassing chapter title like "Understand the Feline Hierarchy" appeared in a large font so none of the other braless women could see. They weren't looking anyway.

I was eager to learn about cat behavior. If you brought a new cat into your home, your resident cat would perceive the new kitty as a threat. Cats were territorial and would become extremely stressed by the intrusion. To introduce a new cat successfully, keep them separated in different locked rooms for weeks. Let them sniff under the doors to get used to the idea there is another cat nearby. Slowly, over months if possible, wedge the doors open a crack, so they can see each other. Rub socks on their heads and let them sniff and attack the scented socks. Gauge how aggressively they attack the socks.

The chapter stressed patience. Some cats will never like each other. I didn't know this. I saw a flash of my life—chasing cats from one room to another in a cat-patterned bathrobe, spraying ill-behaving cats with a water bottle (but not letting the cats see that I was doing it; it should appear to be an act of God, stressed *Cat vs. Cat*), cat toys filling the cabinets, endless mammograms and ultrasounds and a few uterine biopsies in between.

The waiting room was cold and I was hungry. My name was finally called as I was reading "The Importance of Territory: TURF 101" while crossing and rubbing my arms for warmth. I stood at the machine and lay on the table, submitting to the tests, and every time I felt pain I shut my eyes and saw flashes of the older cat attacking the kitten.

When my tests were done, I was left to wait in the ultrasound room, sitting on a pale blue paper liner. I had continued to read about how to extend your cats' territory by adding vertical platforms. This can help your cats interact more harmoniously, as they can keep a social order. The dominant cat gets up higher and the cat lower in the pecking order stays on the floor.

The doctor walked in and said, "There are several things going on," and I snapped my Kindle case shut in surprise. She described three areas that needed to be biopsied. "It's probably normal fibrocystic changes, considering your age, but I'd like to be sure."

I made my follow-up appointments with the receptionist, who advised me to have all three procedures done in one day. "One right after another. Least invasive to most invasive." She sounded bored, which reassured me in the same way a bored flight attendant did during turbulence—although the phrase *least invasive to most invasive* sounded like a line from a CIA manual on torture.

I spent the next week painstakingly keeping the cats separated and shopping online for an aesthetically appropriate cat tower. I had to carry a tote bag between the rooms with a spray bottle, a can opener, cans of cat food, and a fork. I needed to keep one hand free to grab a cat if one escaped. If I let my diligence slip for a moment, my older cat charged into the bedroom in a flash and pounced on the kitten with fury. After each attack, I'd have to hunt around the room to find the kitten. She'd be curled up on a high shelf in my closet in a basket of socks. She'd be tucked in a shoe under the bed. She'd be jammed behind the air conditioner on the floor of my closet. I'd play with her on my bed while my older cat stuck her paws under the door with her claws extended, growling, hoping to snag some tender kitty flesh.

The kitten was slinky and soft and buzzing with joie de vivre. She'd chase her tail in a frenzy of spinning kitty cyclone and topple over at the end like a rag doll. She'd wiggle around under my armpit while I took a nap, purring deep-throatedly on my breast. Her little white paws looked like she had mischievously gotten into a tub of white paint.

"Paint paws! Bunny feet!" I'd stare into her bright green eyes. She'd hold my gaze for a moment, then leap on the curtains and hang like a kitty Tarzan.

I tried to play with my older cat in the other room but she just sat there, staring at the door to the bedroom like a sociopath. If I tried to hold her, she bit me. Behind her golden eyes were the letters K–I–L–L. I was starting to worry this wasn't going to work out.

The older cat was found in the snow outside Key Food on Seventh Avenue. She was pregnant, and the person who found her had said to her, "If you are still here in the snow when I have finished my shopping, I will rescue you." After the woman finished her shopping, the cat was still there waiting in the snow, "as if she had heard me."

At least that's what the cat's bio said on Petfinder.com. It made a good story, anyway, and when I adopted her I told her, "You will never have to get pregnant and live in the snow again." At night when she crawled onto the bed next to me and suckled the blanket, I would coo, "Does Mommy miss her babies?" They'd had to abort her babies due to an infected uterus. In the beginning she, too, had had a shaved belly and a surgical scar.

I returned to the hospital for my biopsies. The first two least invasive procedures were unexpectedly painful, and in the middle of the second least invasive procedure I started to cry. The nurse asked if there was anyone in the waiting room she could get for me and when I remembered that I had come alone I shook my head and tried to pull myself together. When the doctor and nurse finished, I had a surgical bandage on each breast. I went to the bathroom to cry in private. I was so hungry and anxious that I got on my knees and asked God to give me the strength to go through the most in-vasive procedure. I wasn't sure I believed in God but I was desper-ate. I washed my face and pulled up my hair in an elastic band. I walked out of the bathroom and told the nurse I was hungry and she gave me some graham crackers and juice. She told me that my hair looked nice. She finished going over my medical records while I ate my graham crackers like a starving animal. There were crumbs under me on the exam room floor.

"Oh, don't worry about that," she said. "We'll have to clean up worse than that after your procedure anyway."

She found the line for allergies on my record. "Hmmmm, it says here you have an allergy to alcohol?"

"Yes." I was trying to suck the juice out of the juice box with the miniature straw, but the juice could barely flow through the tiny opening.

"What happens when you have alcohol?" she asked, perplexed.

"I get drunk," I said.

It took her a minute.

"Oh, I got it! I've seen this before! Don't you worry about a thing."

She showed me the machine with a vacuum attached to a hollow needle that would be inserted deep into my breast while I lay on my stomach on a table similar to a bunk bed with my neck cranked to the side. My breast would be pulled through a hole and clamped between glass, and a doctor would sit under the table and make a cut to insert the needle. She explained she would need to inject my breast multiple times with lidocaine—"load it up with lidocaine" is what she said—as the area was deep inside.

"It's just like novocaine," she said. "Just not for your teeth."

 When I left the hospital after my three procedures, I had three bandages on different areas of my breasts. The most invasive procedure was harrowing. How sheltered had I been in my life that a standard procedure that millions of women had every week and that bored the receptionist almost broke my neck, my spirit, my resolve? I didn't think I would make it through, but I did and I was bursting with pride and relief when the nurse helped me get off the high table, holding gauze over my breast, which was now bleeding and missing some tissue from deep in its core. I stepped over the bloody gauzes and graham cracker crumbs to get to my flimsy wraparound gown. I went home to await the test results. I thought the worst was over—except for the cats.

The modern, multicolored, stackable-cube cat climber was delivered by UPS the following day, and I had to ask the UPS man to help me get it upstairs. I opened the box and assembled it, trying not to use my left arm so as to avoid pulling on the passageway through my breast left by the tissue-sucking vacuum. The older cat wouldn't climb it and the new kitten seemed trepidatious. I unstacked and restacked the cubes to make two shorter towers. I lay on my bed after the exertion of assembling, disassembling, and reassembling the cat climber. I wanted to rest before I had to leave for my friend's birthday party. My breasts were yellow, green, and blue; the cats were fighting under the bed; and the window was rattling in the wind—the window was shattered and duct-taped back together from when my cat sitter broke it.

That is when I got the phone call. I had to strain to hear the doctor over the catfight and banging windowpane. The result from the most invasive biopsy was DCIS, otherwise known as ductal carcinoma in situ, or early-stage breast cancer. The doctor noted that my cells were high aggression and she referred me to a cancer surgeon. She finished the call saying it could be worse, a lot worse.

I canceled going to my friend's birthday party and got on the internet. My shock multiplied as I read that the treatment of choice for DCIS was often a single or double mastectomy. The cancer surgeon would need to look at my results and recommend treatment. If the DCIS was in one location of the breast, the recommended course of treatment would be a lumpectomy. Often this procedure had no body-altering impact and could or could not be followed by drug therapy and radiation. If the DCIS was in more than one location of the breast, the recommended course of treatment would be a mastectomy followed by drug therapy, breast reconstruction, depression, even more dating trauma, body image issues, endless follow-up appointments, support groups, and a lifetime of psychotherapy.

The next day the news went from terrible to horrific. My friend's boyfriend had killed himself the previous night, the night of her birthday party, the night I got the cancer diagnosis. She was celebrating at a friend's house without him, because they were in the middle of breaking up. My friend found him hanging in their bedroom when she returned in the morning. I could almost feel the cancer spreading as I counted the days until I saw the surgeon.

The cancer surgeon looked like a college freshman who played rugby. She told me within minutes that my cancer was small and localized. The recommended course of treatment was a lumpectomy. She would cut a half-moon under my nipple and follow the guide wire that would be pushed in earlier to point to the tiny spot of cancer. Then she would cut out the cancer. I was beyond ecstatic. I swore to myself that I would never take my breasts for granted again. The cancer surgeon told me to schedule an MRI as a precaution, so she could take a good look at both breasts to make sure there were no other spots of cancer, but she said she didn't expect to find anything new.

THE DAY BEFORE my friend's boyfriend's memorial, I was at NYU's Perlmutter Cancer Center for my MRI. I had fixed my makeup before I left home with the optimistic thought that maybe I would meet a cute guy, perhaps with prostate cancer, who also had an MRI scheduled that day. He would have something early stage also, very treatable—I wasn't interested in dating someone past stage 1. It would be good also if he liked cats so he could comb the new kitten with a flea comb while I distracted the older cat from attacking her. I suspected the new kitten had fleas.

While I was in the waiting room I remembered that it was a women's cancer care center, no hot guys with minimally invasive cancer in sight. Just old ladies, once I really started looking—lots and lots of old ladies who left trails of crumpled Kleenexes, half-sipped water bottles, lipstick-smeared paper cups, canes hooked over armrests, and walkers parked in open areas. Not even any hot young women with cancer, never mind the guys.

The waiting room was packed. All the old ladies had canceled yesterday due to the icy streets. Today, though, they were back with their orthopedic rubber boots, vinyl purses, and *Glamour* magazines. Cell phones were ringing endlessly as the old ladies forgot them on their seats, couldn't find them in their purses, or didn't know how to turn off the ringers anyway.

When I was called in, I thought fleetingly that maybe the MRI tech would be a hot guy. She wasn't, and she had a hard time getting in my IV. She had to call in the nurse, who told me I had thick skin.

She pinched some of the skin on my hand and said, "Thick skin—that's good for you. Less wrinkles."

They left me alone in the room while they sponged down the MRI machine from the previous person who had lain on it with a cancer diagnosis. The chair I waited on was vinyl and had a small rip in the upholstery under my thigh that hurt when it scratched my bare skin. I squirmed in the seat, fearful about my threshold for pain. Then I wondered if my kitty had fleas and whether I'd have to fumigate my apartment.

The MRI machine was a cross between a medieval torture rack and some alien probe table. I was laid on my stomach with my breasts pulled through holes in the beige plastic surface and clamped down tight below. My arms were pulled over my head. My face was stuffed in an inset—I could see only blurred edges of beige plastic and paper liners. There was another needle inserted into my arm and they said at some point there would be a timed injection. They placed a large plastic syringe in my left hand to hold—over my head and resting on the table—as if I were going to self-inject, but my hand was functioning only as a holder.

"The machine has a timer that will activate midway through the MRI and the syringe will empty into your arm. You might feel cold at the injection site. Then you might feel nauseated." The test hadn't even started and my fingers holding the syringe were going numb from my arms being over my head. "Then you might stop breathing," they added, "but that doesn't happen often." They continued, "If you do stop breathing, then you can squeeze the rubber ball."

They unfurled my right fist and I felt a rubber ball placed in my palm and they curled my fingers around it. I couldn't see its color since my face was pressed into the inset and my breasts were pinned, so there was no way to move my head, but I imagined the rubber ball was red, like a clown's nose.

The nurses spoke like a cross between sorority sisters and robots—droning but perky. "If you squeeze the rubber ball, we will ask you, 'Are you sure you wanted to squeeze the rubber ball?' And if you squeeze it again we will stop everything and pull you out." My fingers stiffened around the syringe in my left fist and the rubber ball in my right. They continued, "And if we stop everything and pull you out, then you will have to come back tomorrow and try to do it again."

After twenty minutes I started praying to God to help me not squeeze the rubber ball. I thought about the old ladies who didn't know how to use cell phones. How did they do this? How could they even put their arms over their heads? Was I weak? I was sure of it. Was I a coward? I knew it. Was I going to get through this? I wasn't sure anymore.

I kept counting down from ten. I could barely make out Amy Winehouse on the headphones they'd placed on my ears after sucking and clamping my breasts under the table. The machine made the most god-awful techno slamming ringing noise in staccato patterns. The table was shaking. This was how they would torture and kill people in the future Holocaust on Pluto. Amy Winehouse was singing, "I don't want to go to rehab, no, no, no," and I was praying with sweat rolling down my crushed face: Please don't let me squeeze the rubber ball. God, please, no ball, no rehab, no way, no, no, no.

As I was walking to my friend's boyfriend's memorial the next day, my phone rang. I recognized the number. I pulled over on the sidewalk and took off my mittens. The air was cold. My hands were shaking. The cancer surgeon's first words were "I'm sorry." They had found another spot on the MRI. I would have to return tomorrow for another MRI, this time while they used the hollow-needle attached to a vacuum to suck out more tissue.

"If it's more cancer, is the lumpectomy still an option?" I asked. My fingers were freezing and the wind was howling. I strained, thinking it would be difficult to hear, but I could hear the surgeon clearly when she said, "No. A lumpectomy would no longer be an option." She didn't say what the new option would be, but I knew that she knew that I knew that the new option was a mastectomy.

I sat with another friend on a wooden bench three rows behind my friend's boyfriend's parents. The parents sat in front facing the urn filled with their son's ashes. The green urn was large and looked heavy. It looked uterine-like, with a narrow bottom that gracefully swelled at the top with a large curved handle on each side. My friend's boyfriend had been a very solid, muscular man. His calves were notably large from working out, and many of his grieving friends commented on his calves in their eulogies. I could not conceive that his body was in the jar.

My friend was crying. I wondered how my coat would lie on my chest with one breast. I stared at everyone's breasts as the line formed to hug my friend's boyfriend's parents. When I hugged my friend's boyfriend's mother I told her that her son always made me feel special and loved. She would not let me go. She kept saying over and over, "We didn't know he had so many friends. We didn't know. We didn't know."

On the way home I called an older woman from my alcohol and drug addiction recovery meeting. My voice was loud and high and fast and I didn't recognize it as my own. She recited from the signs on the wall in our meetings to try to calm me down, but she added her own phrases and terms of endearment:

"One day at a time, honey."

"You are not alone, sweetheart."

"Take it easy, darling."

Then she added, "Call the surgeon and ask her to prescribe a Valium."

This was not a slogan on one of our signs at our alcohol and drug addiction recovery meetings. She was a recovering pill addict, so I was relieved that even she thought a Valium was in order. I felt new hope. I called back the surgeon, who agreed to my request and phoned in the prescription. On the way to the pharmacy I bought birdseed to lure sparrows to my window for the cats' entertainment. When I picked up the prescription, I saw there were two pills in the bottle and the instructions read, "Take one a half hour before the procedure, and one after the procedure, if needed." I wondered if I'd need to take the second pill. I had no question about the first.

That night I called multiple friends from my alcohol and drug addiction recovery meetings and described the procedure I would have in the morning in detail. I was hysterical by the time I got to the part where they turned on the tissue-sucking vacuum. Lisa with Gray Hair—we called her that so as not to confuse her with Depressed Lisa, and because we don't use last names—told me to stop calling people and describing the procedure. We hung up and I threw birdseed out the window. There was no sign of birds. I played with the kitty while the older cat watched unblinkingly.

"You can do it, kitty! Get the mousey!"

The kitten pounced on a toy mouse and the older cat pounced on the kitten. The older cat went for the kitten's neck and there was screeching as they tumbled and hissed and snarled and shrieked under the bed. I ran to rescue the kitty, and the older cat emerged with a tuft of fur sticking out of her mouth. I took the kitten in the bedroom with me. I felt a wave of relief when I looked at the bottle with the two Valium on my desk.

I remembered that before they placed me in the MRI yesterday, they had asked if my pants had a zipper and when I said yes they made me remove them. I found a pair of floral stretchy pants with no zipper and laid them out to wear in the morning. I pulled my heavy rubber boots out of the closet because there was snow predicted in the early hours and I had a new terror of falling down and smashing my traumatized breast tissue on the icy sidewalk. I placed the boots by the floral pants. I pulled a flannel shirt that buttoned up the front off a hanger and folded it on top of the floral stretchy pants. They didn't match each other, but that was not a priority. It was soft flannel and easier to put on than a shirt that pulled over the head. I topped the pile with a lime-green jog bra for extra support. The kitten jumped on top of the lime-green jog bra, purring, the toy mouse still in her mouth. I went into the kitchen and made a peanut butter and jelly sandwich and placed it in a Tupperware container.

The next morning while my older friend from recovery whom we called Older Gail sat in the waiting room, I was escorted to the MRI room. They took away my sandwich but let me keep my pants on. I asked one of the sorority-robot techs if she could talk to me in a reassuring voice throughout the procedure.

"I am very anxious," I added so she'd feel sorry for me.

She'd heard this before. "Honey, we'd be worried if you weren't."

I closed my eyes, even though I couldn't see much anyway, and as the machine started to squeal and screech I felt a curtain of peace descend over me. I thought I was having a spiritual experience— that I had found God in the center of an MRI machine and deep down in the tissues of my greatest fears. Then I remembered the

Valium and realized it must have kicked in and either way, God or Valium, I was sure I would make it through this.

There were syringe injections, needle placements, loads and loads of lidocaine, and reassuring voices. "Wow, you are doing great. You're going to feel a pinch. You are okay. You're going to feel an injection. You are the best. This is the worst part. You did great. You are going back in the MRI."

When they pulled me out of the MRI for the last time and removed the needle, they forgot to tell me it was over. I was still pinned to the table, breasts clamped underneath, while they tossed things to each other over my back and talked about their plans for the evening. I heard them cleaning up the bloody paper liners under my breast.

Finally, my voice muffled from inside the inset and rising in pitch, I said, "Excuse me! Excuse me! Are we done?"

"What? Oh yes, great job!"

Someone patted me on the back. They released the clamps on my breasts and awkwardly helped me up to a sitting position. I was so grateful for the sight of my floral stretchy pants in the midst of all the beige plastic, light blue paper liners, and scuffed beige walls. They peeled off their latex gloves and threw them into a medical waste container. I cringed at the sight of the overflowing can, picturing rivers and lakes clogged with latex.

They led me up the back stairs to wait for a mammogram, with my bandaged breast and the container with the one remaining Valium in my gown pocket. I was filled with love for my fellow old lady comrades in the waiting room, with their mismatched tops and loudly patterned stretchy pants. I was in love with my floral stretchy pants. I was high for the first time in seven years and it was awesome.

After the mammogram I went downstairs and showed the bottle with the one remaining Valium to Older Gail, the ex–pill addict. "I don't think I need this last Valium and I'm certainly not giving it to you!" We laughed as I walked over to the trash, shook the pill out into my palm where she could see it, and slowly tipped my palm until it fell into the trash can overflowing with granola bar and sandwich wrappers. Older Gail applauded and the woman sitting next to her asked me how quickly the Valium worked. She was clutching her prescription bottle and was crying. She was young like me. Older Gail told me later that the woman had a fast-moving, invasive breast cancer. They thought it had spread to her other organs. She was waiting for her PET scan. I thought of the Valium sitting on top of the trash. I recalled the doctor saying when she gave me my diagnosis that it could be worse, a lot worse.

Older Gail and I parted ways at the exit to the Cancer Center. The snow was starting to fall as I walked to the subway. I had my backpack on only my right shoulder. My black rubber boots felt solid. I had bought groceries the day before and for extra measure had ordered three full meals of Chinese takeout and packed the Tupperware containers in the fridge. The weather people were excitedly predicting a blizzard. It was Friday, so at the end of the day the labs would close for the weekend. I'd have to wait until Monday to find out if I would lose my breast.

The snow was falling steadily by the time I emerged in Brooklyn. I let the kitty out of the bedroom and the older cat chased her back in, then stretched out on the threshold, languorous and watchful, like the kitty's sadistic prison guard. I tried to activate the chemical ice pack they'd sent me home with. After ringing it in the middle like someone's neck, I threw it away and got out a bag of frozen corn from the freezer. I had bought some frozen vegetables for this reason. I iced my breast while watching romantic comedies and yelling at the older cat.

"Be nice! Stop it! Settle down!"

After they made love, Hugh Grant asked Julia Roberts where she got her perfect breasts. I went to the freezer to swap the warm pack of corn with frozen peas. I wondered if Hugh Grant was too shallow to love a woman with one breast. I still cried when they broke up and then cried again when they got back together. It closed with a scene of her pregnant, lying in his arms on a park bench, her breasts accentuated in an empire-waist dress.

Between *Notting Hill* and *Beauty and the Briefcase*, I opened the window to throw more birdseed on the sill. The air was cold and the snow wet my face. I felt the small hairs coming out of each pore, each snowflake that hit my skin, and my heart thumping under the frozen peas, the bandage, and the traumatized breast tissue. I felt oddly alive and wondered if the birds would come.

Between *Beauty and the Briefcase* and *I Hate Valentine's Day*, I imagined a surgeon with a hacksaw sawing off a breast on a chopping block. I pictured lying on Dr. Frankenstein's table as he sewed the breast of a dead woman on my chest. I saw the bulky stitches, the discolored flesh, the missing nipple. I finally brought myself to image-search mastectomy scars on the internet, and I studied the neat incision line. The images of mastectomy scars were linked to images of mastectomy tattoos of flowers and birds, which ignited my interest. I could finally get a tattoo with great meaning. I read about "going flat," a choice by women to remove both breasts and forgo the breast reconstruction. Some got a tattooed tank top or lacy bra, as if they were wearing the lingerie.

I looked at the big breasts under the soft sweaters of the lead woman in *I Hate Valentine's Day* and imagined what she'd look like flat. Between *I Hate Valentine's Day* and *The Wedding Date*, I checked on the duct-taped window in the bedroom. The wind rattled the crooked frame and the snow was starting to cover the cracks. I worried it might blow in during the storm, but it held.

I called my friend Shauna with Red Hair to tell her about my mastectomy tattoo ideas. Then I called my friend whose boyfriend had killed himself. She said he had looked scary when she found him hanging from their bedroom door. She couldn't believe it was true. She had wanted to take a picture when she found him because she knew that later she wouldn't believe it had really happened. She didn't think it would be respectful to him at the time, but now she wished she had.

"I could choose whether or not to look at the picture, but I think it would have been nice to have it, so I had the choice. I just can't believe that this is true."

The weekend was a whiteout of snow, Chinese food, romantic comedies, catfights, and mastectomy tattoo designs. The city noise was absent as all drivers were banned from the roads. At night, in the silence, my breast throbbed. I couldn't lie on my left side. I lay awake trying to figure out how I would feed the cats after surgery if I couldn't get out of bed. I could get a large Tupperware container and place it by my pillow filled with Chinese food, cat food, a spray bottle, dishes, and chemical ice packs. I broke down and called Lisa with Gray Hair. She told me that if I couldn't get out of bed, she would feed the cats. I asked her: If I needed to have a mastectomy, could I have another Valium before?

"Definitely," she said.

On Saturday night, my phone rings and I recognize the number from the Cancer Center. It is a male nurse who hasn't gotten the memo that my lumpectomy may no longer be an option. He is calling to go over my medical records for the surgery. I fill him in that I am now waiting to see if the surgery will be a lumpectomy or a mastectomy. A pain shoots through my breast as I say the word *mastectomy*.

"That's okay," he says. "Let's go over your medical history for the, let's call it, 'to be determined' surgery."

"Okay," I say.

"Let's see, it says here you had uterine fibroids removed by myomectomy two years ago?"

"Yes, that's correct."

"And it says here that you are bipolar?"

"Yes," I say, somewhat taken aback.

"And it says that you suffer from anxiety?"

"Yes," I say, my heart starting to pound.

"And you suffer from depression?"

"Not all the time," I say, my hands sweating and ears ringing.

"And you are an alcoholic?"

My face turns red but he can't see. I am overcome with shame by my medical records.

"Yes, but I've been in recovery for seven years," I say, on the verge of tears.

There is a pause on his end. "Hold on, honey," he says, "let me close my door."

I can hear him get up and walk across the floor and shut his door. I'm panicking that he will recommend canceling the surgery because he has discovered that I am totally insane. He gets back on the phone.

"Look, sweetie. I'm a recovering alcoholic too, and bipolar, and suffer from depression and anxiety."

"Oh my God, really?" I start to cry with relief.

"Don't you worry about a thing. I am going to take good care of you when you come in for your surgery. You just ask for your friend Jeff and I'll be right there. By the way, it says here your anesthesiologist is Dr. Virk, and he's totally hot."

"Finally, a hot male doctor!"

"Yeah, I mean Dr. Virk can stick a needle in my arm and put me to sleep anytime!"

We both giggle about hot Dr. Virk.

"I don't usually reveal my personal stuff to patients," he says, "but I felt compelled to tell you for some reason."

I am overwhelmed with gratitude for my guardian angel Jeff, the bipolar, alcoholic nurse, and sleep well even if it's only on my right side.

In the morning the cats stop chasing each other. They spot the bird before I do. The older cat flattens her ears and makes the clicking, gurgling noises I imagine Satan makes right before he eats children. The kitten also flattens her ears and chirps. They crouch down level with the windowsill so as to not be spotted. They are sitting side by side, united by a common purpose, which would be murder in the first degree if the window were open. I hide behind the curtain. We all watch, as the snow accumulates and the birds land on the sill. They are little sparrows with puffed-up breasts. They flicker their wings in the snow looking content, frisky. Twittering, they peck in the snow at the seeds. All three of us are watching together, fascinated. The snow continues to fall and I watch as the older cat nuzzles and licks the kitten's cheek. We all look back at the window and watch as furry breasts rise and fall, fly and land, soundlessly, in a perfectly and pristinely soft white world.

Valerie Hegarty is a Brooklyn-based visual artist and an emerging writer. She has been recognized for her achievement in the arts by numerous grants from the Tiffany Foundation, the Rema Hort Mann Foundation, the Pollock-Krasner Foundation, and the New York Foundation for the Arts. She exhibits her artwork internationally and has been awarded residencies from the Marie Walsh Sharpe Art Foundation, Smack Mellon, LMCC, Performance Space 122, Yaddo, and the MacDowell Colony.

EDITOR'S NOTE

I initially received this story from Kikuko Tsumura's translator Polly Barton, and upon first reading I strongly felt that Tsumura's was a voice I wanted to publish in the magazine. The story made me laugh because its emotional landscape felt so true to me, even though I have never experienced the specific situation of the protagonist. Rendered beautifully in Barton's translation, Tsumura's prose is necessarily unadorned, giving the reader precise space to glimpse the tensions that ripple below the surface of the ordinary.

I am grateful to Barton for bringing this piece to us, as well as for her wonderful translation. I would like to share this from Barton on why she chose to translate this story: "I'm really enamored by the way that Tsumura-san creates a voice and an inner world, and . . . find[s] the interest and the poignancy in very mundane and unremarkable experiences. She doesn't really stick to what she knows but is often taking elderly men or other surprising characters as her lens onto the world, which I find admirable. I think her dry, understated humor that sort of suffuses her prose is wonderful, and it makes it a total joy to read and translate. Also I've lived for a while in rural or semi-rural Japan and I felt the story perfectly evoked the quietness of it, the sense that you could fall off the edge of the next street and nobody would notice, juxtaposed with this sense of a very strong-rooted community—so maybe in a way I related to the narrator's outsiderness."

Eleanor Chandler, Managing Editor
Granta

THE WATER TOWER AND THE TURTLE

Kikuko Tsumura

TRANSLATED FROM THE JAPANESE BY POLLY BARTON

THE MOMENT I stepped out of the temple gate, the thick steam wafting over from the building opposite caught in my throat. I knew the source of that steam well enough: udon. The udon manu-factory was right in front of the temple where my parents' graves were.

Tacked up to the wooden wall on the far side of the steam was a recruiting notice. "Experience not required," it read, which was all well and good, but then it said, "Applicants should be sixty-seven years or younger," a stipulation whose peculiar specificity bothered me. Sensing a flash of movement, I looked down to the gutter from where the steam was emanating and saw a single udon noodle slid-ing by. I was quite sure that there used to be more of them in the past. It wasn't clear to me whether the noodles were being deliber-ately abandoned, or if they were the casualties of sheer carelessness, but either way the number going to waste seemed to have dwindled over the years.

This narrow street separating the temple from the udon manu-
factory was on the route I had once taken to school. That was back
in my primary school days, a good few decades ago now. Since
the death of my mother, my last surviving relative in this town,
I came to this area only once every few years to visit the family
grave. Each time I returned, I was surprised to see the udon place
still going.

Yet I did sense they were cutting back a bit, I thought to myself.
Now that I'd started reminiscing about my school days, it struck
me that I might as well walk to my old school. I'd left the temple
at midday, so I still had plenty of time before the furniture would
arrive at my new flat.

Even though there was nothing in particular left for me in this
place where I'd grown up, I'd decided to move back. It had all
started when a former colleague asked if I knew of any nice, repu-
table rooms for rent here. His daughter had a thing about natural
farming and was interested in moving to this considerably more
rural part of the country. I had no leads on any properties what-
soever, but I wanted to be of service if I could, so I'd taken a look
online only to discover that the rent for flats in this area was less
than half what I was paying at the time. In the end, my colleague's
daughter did not take up natural farming: she stopped leaving her
room entirely. Yet I kept thinking about living somewhere for half
what I was currently spending, and before I knew it, I'd moved. As
a single man living alone who'd retired at the stipulated age, there
was really nothing stopping me.

The narrow street that led to where the primary school used
to be was just wide enough for a single car to pass through, and I
spotted several surnames on the nameplates of houses that brought

vague memories of old schoolmates floating to the surface of my mind, but all these names were common to the region, and it was likely that the houses belonged to different people entirely. Not only did I have no relatives here, but it was safe to say I didn't really know anybody in this town at all.

The streets were so quiet. In the city, you'd often catch sight of birds, but their song would be drowned out by the noise of the passing cars. In these streets of my hometown, all I could hear were my own footsteps, and the cries of the sparrows, and some caged bird kept in one of the nearby houses.

It came to me that if I turned down a certain side street, I'd get to the sushi restaurant my parents sometimes got takeaways from on special occasions, but I figured that if I attempted a visit I'd likely only end up lost, so I stuck to the route I knew. Had that restaurant managed to weather these forty-something years? Probably, I guessed, so long as there'd been someone to take over from the sushi master who was there when I was young.

My old school was still there. Not the wooden building I'd been familiar with, of course, but from what I could see, the concrete one that had replaced it was pretty similar in layout to the original. I had no idea when the reconstruction had taken place. Even this concrete number was showing signs of wear and tear. Between the gates and the entrance was a small hut-like structure, with a sign pinned to it that read LOCAL RESIDENTS' PROTECTION SQUAD. Could I join? I wondered. Would the squad accept members without children or grandchildren?

I didn't really feel any deep emotion towards the school, beyond a sense of satisfaction at having seen it again, but when I glanced down the little alley diagonally across from the gates and glimpsed the sea in the distance, I gulped. Now I remembered. This was the same alley I'd gazed down on my way back from school, and at its end, the same sea.

I stood there in the middle of the crossroads for a while, staring out at the strip of sea floating at the end of the alley. Eventually, an approaching car honked its horn ostentatiously at me and snapped me back into reality, and I set off back along the road I'd come down.

Walking towards the town's little train station, served not by the public network but a private line, I started to worry about how few amenities there were around here. How did people get by with just one convenience store? Of course I myself had once coped. But I wanted to know if the convenience store could be relied on, so I went inside and roamed up and down the aisles. Being in the country, I'd feared its selection might be limited, but I soon realized that it was a standard convenience store with the standard array of goods, which comforted me a bit. There was a decent selection of magazines and a range of cheap DVDs, too. I've recently moved to this area, I said to a cashier with a bun and oversized glasses. Where can I go to buy the kinds of books that you don't stock here? Or household tools and that sort of thing?

If you go onto the highway, she informed me politely, there's a big chain bookstore and a home store, and a supermarket as well.

As I pictured the location of my new home in my head, it came to me that the block of flats could be accessed from the highway, and I decided to switch my route so I could investigate.

As the shop assistant had promised, beside the four-lane na-tional road was a large bookshop shaped like a big block of tofu, a rectangular two-story home store painted a dull shade of blue, and, beside it, a one-story supermarket that seemed pretty spacious. They looked rather out of place in this area, where all the other buildings were so diminutive and flat. Perhaps as the result of some kind of financial arrangement, the supermarket and the home store shared a car park, which had a fast-food chain and an all-you-can-eat Korean barbeque restaurant perched in the corner.

Otherwise, there was basically nothing there. Lining the sides of the highway with its meager scattering of cars were fields, houses, a great big billboard advertising termite extermination, a great big billboard advertising a cash loan hotline, a great big billboard advertising flats for sale, and so on. All the billboards were noticeably enormous. That was proof of how much space there was in this part of the country. Had the house I'd grown up in had a termite problem? I wondered about this as I walked down one side of the highway, pulling out my smartphone to check my whereabouts on the map before turning down the road that led to the coast, where my new flat was. Now that I was getting farther from the station there seemed to be more fields around. Not as many as when I'd been growing up, for sure, but the fact that at least half of them had survived came as a shock.

I walked along the side of an onion field facing the highway, heading for the ground floor of the two-story block midway down the road to the sea. Going by rent alone, there was no end of flats in the area that I could have selected, and my sole reason for choosing this one over any of the others was that it was near the house I'd grown up in. And yet when I arrived, I saw that the place as it existed in my memory didn't quite match up with the place as it actually was. Cocking my head in bemusement, I stuck the key that the estate agent had given me into the keyhole.

There'd been a water tower, it came to me suddenly. I couldn't for the life of me remember where, but it was somewhere around here. In the middle of a field, perhaps, or standing in the grounds of somebody's house. It had been a lovely shade of—I don't know if you would call it cyan or pale aqua or what—but in any case it was a beautiful shade of light greenish blue, and there was something about the grandeur of its presence, how it stood taller even than the school, which had captivated me. Whenever I played around with friends outside, I'd steal glances in its direction when they weren't looking. The truth is, I didn't know it was a water tower until later, once I'd grown up. It was with the vague notion that I wanted to build things like that tower that I found myself a job at a construction company with strong connections to the water industry.

I opened the door to my flat and was just about to step inside when I heard a voice at my back.

Um, excuse me? said the voice. It belonged to a middle-aged woman with a surly expression who looked to be just a few years younger than I was. I'm the caretaker here, she said, and, pointing towards the garage, went on: A parcel's arrived for you. Will you deal with it please?

I looked in the direction she indicated, and sure enough I saw the box that she meant: not that deep, but of considerable height and width. I made out the name of the company printed on the box, and hurried towards it, my heart fluttering a little.

The cross bike I'd ordered online had arrived early. She could have sent the courier away, the caretaker told me, but he'd begged her not to make him redeliver such a big parcel, and because she knew the person who ran the company, she'd agreed to sign for it on my behalf.

This really is the countryside, I thought to myself as I listened to

her story. When you know the person who runs the delivery company, you know you're in the countryside.

I'd be grateful if you opened it right away, she said, and before I
could really think, I was saying, Then I'd be grateful if you lent me
a box cutter.

She retreated into her room and emerged with a barber's razor
saying, This'll do, won't it?

The large, flat cardboard parcel was bound together with huge
copper staples, and it took some doing to get it open.

What is that thing, anyway? asked the caretaker, coming up
behind me.

It's a bike, I answered.

Why would you go and order something like that? she asked as
she mounted the enormous piece of discarded cardboard and folded
it in half. That didn't make it much less bulky, though, so I scored
some slits into it with the razor, and somehow managed to fold it
into smaller pieces.

Someone I knew from my previous workplace took up cycling
and he gave me the idea, I told her. He was always saying how much
he enjoyed it.

As I spoke, I recalled the conversation we'd had at my leaving
party. The guy in question was younger than I was but still past
forty, and after being diagnosed with hyperlipidemia, he told me,
he'd taken up exercise.

You're a strange one, you are, the caretaker said, shaking her
head as she picked up the strips of bubble wrap that had been en-
casing the bicycle, winding them round and round into a ball. The
person living in your flat before you was a strange one too. And she
lived on her own, like you.

I couldn't figure out if the caretaker was a real busybody or if she just had a lot of spare time on her hands, but either way, she stood there chatting away as I divested my bicycle of its myriad pieces of packaging.

She was an elderly woman, the caretaker went on, by the name of Noyo. See, even her name was strange! Apparently she'd been in love with some childhood friend of hers. He was a few years older than she was, but he went off to war and never came back and she refused to marry anyone else. She worked selling insurance, made it as far as the head of the branch, if memory serves me right.

Noyo had moved to the area after retiring, the caretaker went on to say, and found herself a job in the clothes alterations kiosk at the local supermarket, where she'd worked right up until the day she died of heart failure. Before Noyo's death, the caretaker had been wary of her, figuring that she was exactly the type of person to die unnoticed in her flat and go undiscovered for months. In the end, the person to find her body was a young colleague of hers from the alterations kiosk.

Noyo, it turned out, had forever been telling people at work that if she ever failed to turn up to the kiosk without giving any notice, they were to go over to check on her. She would always inform them if she couldn't make it into work, and had taught herself how to use a mobile phone in the case of an emergency. When Noyo hadn't come in one day, a colleague had tried to call her, but Noyo hadn't picked up. So I just came over, the young woman had said with a shrug.

Noyo's will had been easy to find, and disposing of her personal affairs was simple enough. She'd instructed that half of her money should go to distant relatives living in another part of the country, and the other half to the closest orphanage.

The caretaker spoke in such detail that I had to wonder if she should be revealing so much to me, given I'd never even met this person, but I supposed she'd decided that it was all right, since the subject in question was dead and had no close relatives. As it happened, I already knew from the estate agent that the previous tenant had passed away in the flat. Would the caretaker talk about me in the same way to the next person, if something happened to me? Well, I thought, so be it.

The only thing is, the caretaker went on, she had this pet turtle, which has proved a real headache. She only got it a couple of months before she died, see, so it wasn't mentioned in the will. I'm keeping it in my room for the moment. Would you like to see it?

But knowing that my furniture would be arriving at any moment, and that afterwards I wanted to take my cross bike for a spin, I declined and said I'd leave the turtle-viewing for another time.

Before you go, there's something I want to ask you, the caretaker said, folding her arms across her chest and looking straight at me. How is it that people like Noyo and you can stand to be all on your own?

I looked down at the caretaker's left hand, verifying the presence of a ring on her wedding finger, and then shrugged. I guess I've always been busy, I said.

But there are plenty of busy people who aren't single, the caretaker replied.

I was busy and I was never very good at any of that stuff, I said, and then I walked into my room cradling large amounts of cardboard and packaging.

As I consigned the rubbish to the corner of the kitchen, my mind traced its way along the path that had led me to where I was now,

the path I so rarely thought of. I realized soon enough that there
was a reason that I so rarely thought of it, and stopped—though
not before I'd had time to recall the woman of twenty-eight my
boss had introduced me to back when I was the same age, who'd
said I was "too vacant." And the woman five years younger than
me I'd been intending to marry at thirty-five, who had turned out to
already be married, and had returned in the end to her emotionally
blackmailing husband. And the woman ten years younger who I'd
met at forty-five, who'd broken it off because of her concern about
the perils of childbirth. At work, I'd found myself being sent all
around the country in place of the married folk whose families prevented them from being posted to far-flung places, and occasionally
I would get friendly with women in one of those various locations,
but usually, whenever it looked like things might be going somewhere, I'd be called back to head office.

It wasn't that I wanted to stay single and carefree. Somehow
things never quite went my way, and I wasn't ever able to plunge
myself headlong into anything. I regret that, I really do. The reason
that people need family and children is that without duty, life just
feels long and flat. The simple repetitiveness becomes too much to
bear.

But those thoughts vanished into the ether with the arrival of
the moving company. The furniture they'd brought from my previous flat consisted of a fridge, a washing machine, a futon, a single
chair, and two storage boxes for clothes. Everything else I planned
to order online.

You must have a sea view from out there, the youngest-looking
of the movers said, pointing to a back-room window whose storm
shutters were still down.

By the time I collected myself and replied, Oh really? the kid had already finished putting on his shoes in the entranceway.

I decided to leave the furniture and the sea for the moment and went back down into the garage to mess around with the cross bike. A clear plastic pouch housed the instruction manual and an Allen key, which I gathered was used to turn the handlebars, which had been rotated to one side in order to fit the bike in the box, as well as to adjust the height of the saddle and so on. I stood to the left of the bicycle as I adjusted the angle of the handlebars, closing each eye in turn, blinking several times, and tilting my body from side to side to check that they were really straight. According to the manual, the part between the handlebars and the frame I'd been adjusting was called the "stem." I'd learned something, I thought to myself.

I went back to my room to pick up my rucksack, packed it with my wallet and the new chain lock that I'd ordered online along with the bike, and set out. Compared to the city bikes I'd ridden before, the "top tube"—another new word from the manual—was much higher, and I had a hard time straddling it and perching on the saddle. After a while I realized that I needed to place my feet on the pedals before trying to sit down. Once I'd figured that out, I managed to set forth in relative comfort, pitching gently from side to side as I went.

Beer, beer, beer, sounded the voice inside my head. My body felt lighter. A bike is not like a car. On a bike you feel the speed right there on your skin.

Under a gazebo in the corner of a field was an unmanned stall selling homemade pickles. Unable to resist, I stopped my bike and bought a bag of pickled aubergines and a whole pickled daikon.

The money went into a small square wooden box at the side of the stall.

Then I set off in the direction of the supermarket once again, the beer, beer, beer chant growing ever stronger. There were very few bikes in the rack. My gaze was drawn to the abnormally chunky blue mountain bike chained up to one side, and I found myself pulling in alongside it. My bike was also blue, as it happened, but compared to that mountain bike it looked like a little boy's. The round white-on-black logo didn't help.

The chorus of beer, beer, beer was now so commanding I couldn't think of anything else. Inside the supermarket I made a beeline for the alcohol section, picked up a well-chilled six-pack of amber Yebisu, marched over to the till, and left.

I'm forgetting something, I thought, cocking my head, but of late I'd given up hating myself for being unable to remember things, and so I simply told myself that whatever it was, I'd come back for it when I remembered. With that, I made my way to the bike rack, where I came across the owner of the mountain bike studiously removing the chain and the other bits of his lock. He was kitted out even more seriously than I'd envisaged: a black helmet, black sunglasses, and a black Lycra outfit. As I stood watching him, whistling internally in awe, the petite, wiry-looking man raised his tanned face. He was almost certainly older than I was, I saw, the kind of age that made him unequivocally an old man. With his long gray-streaked hair tied at his neck and his sunglasses, there was something pretty intimidating about him.

Thinking it wouldn't do to keep ogling him, I averted my eyes, just as he said, That's a great bike you've got!

Oh no, I said, taken aback. No, it's nothing on yours, this is just a cross bike I bought for fifty thousand yen online, it's not a patch on what you've got there, I said, indicating his mountain bike sheepishly.

A cross bike is perfect for this area, though, he said. The roads are really not in great condition.

He had a slight accent—it sounded as if he was from the south, maybe Kyūshū. The accent went a long way to soften the ridiculously professional look created by his cycle gear.

At first I was planning to get a road bike, I said, but I thought I'd try this out for a year and see how it goes.

I used to ride a road bike too, he said, but the roads here are surprisingly uneven and I was forever getting punctures. That's why I switched over to this one, but now the rear hub is quite heavy, and I get tired quickly.

Right, I said, though in my head I was thinking: rear hub, you say? I resolved to look up what that was when I got home.

I'll see you around, the man said, raising a hand and cycling away. He cut a dashing figure, that was for sure. I stood watching him until he left the car park, then zipped the six-pack into my rucksack and cycled back along the highway to my new home.

Dusk was falling. I had the faint sense that it came earlier here than in the flat I was living in before. My head was a lot clearer now that I'd bought the beer, and I recalled something else I'd meant to buy: turtle food. There was another thing as well, though, which I still couldn't remember.

I parked my bike in the rack for the block of flats, and pressed the buzzer for the caretaker.

I'll take the turtle, I told her when she emerged.

Oh, will you? she said, nodding blankly, and then came out

carrying the small tank. I've got a box of food, she told me, so I'll bring that round later. But what made you decide to take it?

This woman questions everything, I thought to myself. In a flash of inspiration, I said that I'd seen Aki Takejo talking about keeping turtles on some TV program a while back and had been wanting one ever since.

Hah. The caretaker laughed darkly.

Back inside my room, I unzipped my rucksack and took out the Yebisu and the bagged pickles.

Ah! I exclaimed, striking myself on the forehead. I should have bought kitchen stuff.

Setting one can of beer and the aubergine pickles aside, I transferred my shopping of the stuff to the fridge. I rinsed my hands, put the pickles and the beer on my chair, which I carried into the back room, and then opened the storm shutters. Just as the guy from the moving company had said, there was indeed a sea view from the balcony. The sea was mottled with the light of the setting sun.

I carried the turtle tank out onto the balcony, washed my hands again, and took the beer and the bag of pickled aubergine off the chair. I'd been planning to take the chair into the back room and drink the beer there, but I decided to move it out onto the balcony instead.

Outside, the sea moved a little closer. I breathed in. The smell! There were probably too many impurities mixed in to really call it the smell of the sea, but it still seemed to me like the same smell I'd breathed as a kid.

And there in the distance, to one side of the balcony, was the water tower I'd been looking for. It was curious that I hadn't been able to see it from the highway, but I supposed these flats must have blocked it from view. There it stood in the middle of the field, delicately assembled of slender metal bones. There was an onion-drying shed nearby, and a wooden gazebo, which I guessed the farmers used as a resting spot.

I popped the tab on the can of beer and raised it to my lips. It tasted so good, it was as if all the cells in my body trembled in appreciation.

I've come home, I thought. Home to this scenery, to all these things I used to look at.

As I raised the beer to my lips a second time, the turtle in the tank moved, and I heard a faint scrape of gravel. The only other sound was that of the wind blowing.

I opened up the bag and took a bite of one of the pickled aubergines. Then I remembered the other thing I'd forgotten to get. Résumé templates, so I could apply for the job at the udon manufactory in front of the temple.

Tomorrow, I decided, I'd go to the supermarket and buy the templates. I'd cycle there—in the morning this time. I was pretty sure that would feel great.

―――――――

Kikuko Tsumura was born in Osaka, Japan, where she still lives today. She has won numerous Japanese literary awards, including the Akutagawa Prize for her book *Potosuraimu no fune* (The Pothos Lime Boat) and the Noma Literary New Face Prize. "The Water Tower and the Turtle" is her first story to appear in English. Her first novel in English, *There's No Such Thing as an Easy Job*, is forthcoming from Bloomsbury.

Polly Barton is a translator of Japanese literature and nonfiction, currently based in Bristol, U.K. Her book-length translations include *Friendship for Grown-Ups* by Nao-Cola Yamazaki, *Mikumari* by Misumi Kubo, and *Spring Garden* by Tomoka Shibasaki. She has translated short stories for *Words Without Borders*, *The White Review*, and *Granta*. After being awarded the 2019 Fitzcarraldo Editions Essay Prize, she is currently working on a nonfiction book entitled *Fifty Sounds*.

EDITOR'S NOTE

What we first found exciting about Willa C. Richards's "Failure to Thrive" was its ambitious use of physicality. The sensory details are visceral, with an economy and a cadence that my colleagues and I could not let go. Everything in this story feels vivid and fully inhabited—the chilly apartment with its sputtering heat, the clammy skin of an ailing mother, the heft of a skull in her hand, the pool water lapping at her body. But that is only the first layer of Richards's ambitious work. Beyond exterior sensation is a more abstract and nuanced exploration of physical being. Richards is interested in the most intimate realities of a human body—not just its condition but one body's desire for or aversion to another, one body's need for another, the remains of bodies from long ago, and the future growth of one small human; she explores this in a way that is detailed and precise, but never either clinical or gratuitous. A third layer, the psychological examination of a tattered relationship, takes place in the tight proximity of a shared blanket, across a diner's booth, in the confines of a compact car blocked in by thundersnow. With a command and poise that would be remarkable for any writer, not just one making her debut publication, Richards brings her characters and their environment together to create a truly unforgettable, unshakeable story.

Emily Nemens, Editor
The Paris Review

FAILURE TO THRIVE

Willa C. Richards

ALICE READ JOHN Mark's letter, her eyes narrowed, as I paced our tiny apartment. The envelope contained instructions for retrieving two sets of human remains from the University of Florida. I sometimes worked for John Mark, the director of the Milwaukee Public Museum, in exchange for modest paychecks and access to the museum's research collection. I often did the jobs the museum interns refused to do, like retrieving artifacts originally accessioned by the MPM from other institutions and bringing them back to Milwaukee. I hadn't taken one of these jobs since before Tess was born, afraid to leave her or Alice, but we were so poor we had begun to eat only the casseroles Alice's mother sent over in weekly batches.

Alice tossed the letter on the coffee table. She wiped a bead of sweat from her forehead. I thought about how sweaty she used to get after her long runs up and down the Beerline. How good her skin tasted. I couldn't remember the last time she'd gone running.

"So you want to go?"

"I don't," she said.

"I'll drop you at your mother's, then."

Alice's mother refused to speak to me because we'd had Tess out of wedlock. Once, she'd called the apartment, and when I picked up the phone, she whispered, You're my penance, William. She loved Tess, it was obvious, but she acted as if Alice were a single mother. Their relationship had become fraught.

"Like hell you will," Alice said.

I threw my hands up. "What then? We need this money."

"Shush," Alice whispered. "You'll wake her." She was right; Tess began then to make low, wet noises from the other room.

I went to get her but Alice said, "She's fine." She wanted Tess to learn to calm herself down. Were babies even capable of that kind of thing?

The windows let too much of the winter into the old apartment. To compensate, we had two space heaters near our orange couch and an electric blanket under which Alice was hunkering. She looked highly flammable. The cold crept up through my sock feet and I started shivering, so I went to the couch and Alice held the blanket up for me to come underneath with her. Even though she kept a whole cushion between us, I was grateful. It reinvigorated my efforts.

"Come with," I whispered.

"Fine," she said. "I'm sick of being here anyway."

"Where?"

She gestured around. The space heaters hummed incriminatingly.

"This crappy apartment. Milwaukee."

"A trip will be good for us," I said. "We can see the ocean, maybe even some mountains on the way?"

She shrugged and I felt a surge of hope.

"Even if we leave, we're still stuck here."

I cringed but said nothing. Though we'd both been born in Wisconsin, I knew Alice had always dreamed of living in some ocean-side city where the weather was less hostile, or at least more

predictable. She said she wanted sunshine every day. But then we
had Tess, the progress on my dissertation slowed to a halt, and
Alice put school on hold indefinitely. Sometimes I was scared she
was right; maybe we were stuck.

The lights flickered and went out. Snow on the power lines. I
wanted to kiss Alice in the dark, but I sat on my hands. Tess's cries
turned into sobs. The lights came back on. Alice went into the bedroom and brought Tess with her to the couch. She tucked herself
back under the blanket and pulled the wide neck of her shirt down
so her breasts fell out. Alice grimaced as the baby took a nipple in
her mouth. I knew they were sore: Alice rubbed cream on them
at night. I missed my own mouth, my own tongue around them.
She used to let me feel their raised edges with my fingertips, which
made her moan. I had no conception of the line between what felt
good and what hurt. I reached for her. The building was quiet except for the sound of water rushing through the pipes.

"Stop," Alice said.

I thought about some of our early sex, when we'd first started
dating. Once I'd playfully swatted at her face and pressed her right
cheekbone hard into the bed with my palm so she couldn't turn
her head or look at me. She said, Hit me, and I'd slapped her so it
made a sick noise. When her face bloomed with my handprint, I got
harder inside her, and I was seized by a rush of guilt.

"Okay," I said, and sat on my hands again.

The lights went off again and the radiator gasped. Tess fell asleep
with the nipple still in her mouth and I watched Alice fight sleep,
her head lolling back on the couch, her shirt pulled low, the darkness filling in her collarbone and the hollow spaces of her throat.

———

TESS SCREAMED. SHE woke every two hours. Did she hate the world already? Did she miss the womb? Did she hate me? Alice said babies just screamed. This was normal. This was natural. I was learning how to do things in the dark. I was learning how to do things in my sleep. I pulled the baby away from Alice and her eyes stayed closed, but I knew she wasn't sleeping. Sometimes we let each other lie about that sort of thing. She looked vulnerable with her breasts out and Tess gone from her chest. The winter sky was heavy with purple light and it flooded the apartment, shadowed Alice, bruised her body. I changed Tess in the dark and put her back on Alice and Alice held our baby as if I'd never taken her, as if she'd been there all along.

TESS WAS A breech baby. She was also a very large baby, which the doctors informed us was an affliction, one they called fetal mac-rosomia. I had scrawled these words, the question of them—fetal macrosomia?—in my field notebook with the hopes of determining their full meaning later. I sometimes did this with potsherds with-out proveniences, too. Alice ignored the words. She disliked her doctors, all of whom were young men, and she only barely trusted our midwife.

The contractions forced Tess against Alice's pelvic bones for twelve hours until the midwife could turn her. The doctors said Alice would need an episiotomy, a procedure they described as mostly a preventive measure. They made a surgical cut in Alice's vagina in anticipation of tearing. This seemed to me emblematic of medicine in general; doctors were always trying to do the body's work themselves. The cut ruptured and became a third-degree tear. Tess was born faceup and Alice received twenty-two stitches. The midwife said it was normal to tear, natural, but she conceded that twenty-two was a lot.

At one point, during a particularly painful contraction, Alice swung her legs over the side of the hospital bed and kicked me in the shin. She said she wanted to break my nose. I said okay and let her punch me, and though she did not break my nose, it bled. When I leaned over her in the hospital bed to kiss her temple, she wiped some of my blood away with the back of her hand. In the weeks after Tess was born, I thought of this moment often.

WE LEFT FOR Florida as soon as the streets were clear and salted. Alice stared out the window and Tess screamed. When I couldn't drive anymore I stopped at a Big Boy in southern Indiana. Alice was pretending to sleep with her head against the window and I shook her shoulder. She threw my hand off.

"I'll stay in the car," she said.

"No. Come eat."

I got out and grabbed Tess, still in her car seat, from the back. I swung the car seat between my legs, a motion that had calmed her before. But when I swung the seat forward she flew out of it, and her body was in the air for an interminably long time before she fell into a deep snowbank. I stood for a second and then rushed to her. She made no noise and her eyes were wide as though she might even smile. I picked her up and held her to me, brushing the snow off her snowsuit. I kissed her tiny nose. I said, "Sorry, sorry," though it struck me as something you say to an adult, someone who understands regret. Alice got out of the car.

"Why didn't you buckle her into the seat?" I asked.

"Why didn't you?"

I wanted to put my hands on her. Instead I held Tess tighter.

The restaurant was sticky—the linoleum floors, the plastic table-cloths, the menus. I had to peel myself off everything I touched. I ordered the buffet for both of us and made up a plate of eggs and bacon and waffles for Alice, even though I knew she'd barely touch it. She'd had almost no appetite since Tess was born and I'd watched her shrink, burning thousands of calories nursing but barely eating.

Alice picked at her food until Tess started crying again. I knew Tess was probably hungry by now and I tried to finish eating but I felt the whole restaurant watching us. Tess cried and we left her in her seat, each waiting for the other to pick her up. People stared. Alice put her head down on the table.

I HAD THOUGHT the warm air and the change of scenery might cheer Alice, but the farther south we went, the more deflated she became. We stopped that night in Chattanooga, and even though I pointed out the smoky silhouettes of the Appalachian foothills outside our hotel window, she called the city a total dump. We left early the next morning, and by the time we got to Gainesville she looked withered. The hair at the back of her neck was damp. I rolled the windows down and she rolled them back up again.

I dropped the girls off at the motel and went to pick up the bones. The skeletons were housed in the anthropology department, which was in the social sciences building, a structure that looked as if it had been built with a nuclear holocaust in mind.

I gave the department secretary John Mark's card and she went to get the head of Collections, a professor named Dr. Sherman. I was surprised, and then a little ashamed, when a tall, very tan woman, in khaki shorts and a denim button-up, introduced herself.

She dusted her hands on the bottom of her shirt, and we shook. I followed her to Collections, which was in the basement.

I wondered if all museum basements were exactly the same—full of things curators didn't want anyone to see but couldn't get rid of. Human remains, especially ones with problematic proveniences, often fell into this category. In the middle of the basement there was a makeshift room, made of plywood, with a lock on the door and a handwritten sign that said KEEP OUT. Dr. Sherman unlocked the flimsy door and went inside. As the sign directed, I kept out. She came back with a cardboard Kinko's box. She hummed as she inventoried its contents. I checked her work against the accession sheet John Mark had given me.

"All good, yeah?" Dr. Sherman asked.

"Uh, I don't know," I said. "John Mark said this burial had one adult female and one juvenile—you've only got the adult female."

Dr. Sherman knitted her brow and checked the notes. She went back into the plywood room and shuffled around for a while before she came out again, empty-handed.

"Well, you're right, but I can't find her," she told me. "Why don't you just take this gal for the time being." She gestured at the skeleton. "Come back tomorrow for the other one?"

"I have to leave tomorrow."

"Well, that's a shame," she said.

"Why's that?"

"It's no problem—we'll get you the little one. Just gotta track 'em down."

"Yeah, all right." I wrote down the motel phone number on an index card. "Call if you find it today? I can come back later."

She smiled; her lips were a lovely shape. I packed the bones up carefully, and then I shook Dr. Sherman's hand and I imagined for a second what those long, tan fingers would feel like in my mouth. I dropped her hand.

"You've got nice hands," I said.

"Thanks," she said. She picked up the card and folded it in half, working the crease between her thumb and forefinger.

BACK AT THE motel, I slid the box underneath the desk. Truth be told, of the two of us, Alice was the actual osteologist. I knew enough to get by, but she had been studying bioarchaeology before Tess, and she was already a qualified skeletal analyst. Once I'd watched her excavate a historic burial with a set of bamboo tools she'd made herself. Though a construction crew had truncated the grave with a large pipe, Alice took care to recover every bone that was left. I loved watching her work so much that eventually our crew chief noticed and threatened to dock my pay. Alice cackled at his reprimand. Yeah, get back to work, asshole, she shouted at me from across the site. I gave her the finger. The crew rolled their eyes at our attempts to flirt.

I locked the room and went to find the girls. Alice was at the pool, stretched out on a white plastic chaise. Tess squirmed on her stomach. Alice wore a black bikini and her body looked different to me. She used to walk around the apartment in nothing but her socks just to drive me crazy; she had always been easy in her skin. But I hadn't seen her like this in a while; I hadn't seen her naked much at all. She had the straps of her top pulled down so her shoulders were bare and her clavicles were so sharp it hurt to look at them. I could see her ribs, too, stretched out as she was. She was wearing heart-shaped sunglasses that swallowed her face and made

her look like a curly-haired cartoon. I wished I could take a picture
of her because I was consumed, for a moment, by the feeling that I
was on the brink of losing her completely. She waved for me to sit
down next to her, which tore me from my thoughts.

I sat down in the chair next to hers, but she stood up abruptly and
put Tess in my arms. Then she dove into the deep end of the pool.
When she surfaced she swam back over and spat a thick stream of
water at us. Tess screamed and I jostled her like, It's okay, it's okay.

"I have to go back in the morning," I told her.

Alice put her elbows on the edge of the pool and looked up at me.
"Why?"

"They've lost the little one and they're still trying to track it
down."

Alice tilted her head back so the sun shone on her throat and all
her hair floated on the pool's surface behind her.

"We could go see the ocean after. If you want?" Oceans, like
mountains, used to have a certain effect on Alice's state of mind.

"The pool's just fine," she said.

She spat at us again and then she dipped quietly under the water
and I waited for her to come up, but instead she swam the length of
the pool and stayed underwater for what felt like minutes.

IT WAS LATE when the phone rang. Too late. Alice and I were on the
bed with a good foot between us. I had thought she was sleeping
but she grabbed the phone fast.

"Hello?"

"Hello? Is William there?" I heard Dr. Sherman's voice.

"No." Alice hung up the phone.

"That was for work, Alice!" I shouted. "She's the head of Collections."

"And? What in the hell is she calling for at this hour?"

I shrugged; I had no answer for that.

"You asshole," Alice said.

I tried to go to her but she pushed me away. The curls at her temple were damp. I wanted to touch her forehead but she turned away from me and put her pillow over her head.

I WOKE UP hard. I reached for Alice, found her hand, and put it on my dick. She held me for a minute, cupping my balls. She let Tess scream and I wanted to fuck Alice so bad, but then she went to Tess and plucked her from the hotel's borrowed crib. She fed her on the edge of the bed and I just lay there thinking about Alice's body in the pool and about peeling that wet suit from her skin and tasting her. I sat up in bed hoping to pull her in to me, but I jolted backward when I saw the skull from the box grinning at me from across the room.

"Jesus," I said.

Tess cried out.

"William!" Alice shouted. "She was almost asleep."

She turned back to me. I motioned at the skull on the desk.

"What's that doing out?"

"I was looking at it," she whispered. "I was curious."

"About what?"

"Never mind. I just forgot to put it away is all."

The floodlights from the parking lot outside filtered through the blinds and cast striped shadows on Alice and Tess, the bed, the skull. The sutures on top of the cranium gleamed and seemed to eat all the light in the room. I hurried to put it back inside the box, which I slid under the desk again. Alice glared at me with Tess still attached to her nipple. It occurred to me I was going crazy; I felt a heat emanating from her breasts. I reached out and touched them and they were hot beneath my fingertips. Then I put the back of my hand on her forehead and it came away wet.

"You're sweating," I told her.

"Obviously." She wiped her temples and then put Tess on me and went into the bathroom where I heard her throw up. She flushed the toilet. When she started throwing up again I collected Tess's things and threw on some clothes. I found the phone book under the Bible in the bedside table.

When Alice came out from the bathroom, I told her we were going to the doctor. She didn't protest. Her hair hung in limp curls, some of them plastered to her skull so I could see the shape of her head, like the cranium in the box.

AT THE HOSPITAL they pumped her full of fluids and antibiotics and also something that knocked her out. I sat in the waiting room, nervously jostling Tess and surveying the pictures on the walls. The hospitals in Wisconsin all have pictures of exotic, mostly tropical locales—Hawaii or Florida or the Caribbean—palm trees and white sand beaches and brightly colored fish swimming through coral. I was surprised to see that the hospitals in Florida had the same photos. They hadn't chosen pictures of the snow-covered forests of northern Wisconsin or the grass plains of Wisconsin's Driftless Area or the shores of Lake Michigan. A doctor touched my elbow gently and I stood up. Tess squirmed awkwardly as I squeezed her against me.

"She's going to be just fine," he said.

I nodded. "Thanks," I said.

"Mastitis is serious but highly treatable."

"Mastitis?"

"Infection and inflammation of the milk ducts."

I made a face.

"With antibiotics and rest she'll be just fine."

I wished he would stop saying the word *fine*.

"When can she go?"

"We'll keep her through the night but she's free to go tomorrow. There's something else, though." The doctor motioned for us to sit. "I'm concerned about Alice's mental health."

"I'm sorry?" My head felt thick.

"I've referred her to a psychiatrist."

The doctor reached out and rubbed Tess's chubby little arm and I instinctively pulled her away.

"Oh," I said. "Okay."

The doctor handed me some pamphlets. "Here's some literature," he said. "Call me if you have questions."

"Alice is . . ." I waited. "Eccentric."

The doctor gave me a heavy look that I thought said, Oh, you poor, dumb fuck. And then he stood and left me alone with Tess and those stupid pictures on the walls.

In the morning, the doctor said they were keeping Alice until midday because she was still dehydrated and also sleep-deprived. Let's be honest, I told him, we're all sleep-deprived. I took Tess with me to the university to inquire about the second box of remains. Dr. Sherman was surprised to see us, which is to say she was surprised to see Tess. On Dr. Sherman's face, I watched myself turn into a completely different person. Neither of us mentioned the phone call.

She brought us into the basement. She'd found the juvenile. I put Tess's car seat on the floor and rocked it with my foot as Dr. Sherman inventoried the skeleton. When she'd counted all seven of the cervical vertebrae and placed them back in the box, she put her hand out to shake mine.

"Where's the cranium?" I asked her.

She checked the sheet.

"Tell John Mark—no cranium," she said.

"No cranium?"

"Well, that's right."

"Okay," I said.

This seemed an appropriate place for an apology but instead Dr. Sherman asked, "You're a doctoral student?"

"Yeah, I'm doing Mississippian ceramics."

"Ah, so you're a pothead," she said.

I smiled like I hadn't heard this joke a thousand times. "Sure." I put the cardboard box under one arm and Tess's car seat under the other.

"Drive safe," Dr. Sherman shouted after us.

WE WENT TO pick up Alice from the hospital. She was ready, back in her own clothes, her bag hanging off one shoulder. When I hugged her, she was limp, and I still felt the heat in her breasts when they pressed against my chest.

"How are you feeling?" I asked.

She moved her lips against my neck. "If you leave me again, I'll kill you."

Alice leaned down to peer through the window. Tess was in the car seat, the box of juvenile bones beside her.

"Jesus, William," she said. "You couldn't have put those in the trunk?"

"Our dig kits are still back there. There's no more room."

"Maybe you should just throw mine away," she said.

"Don't say that."

Alice eased herself into the passenger seat. "Are we going to the ocean?" she asked me.

"What?"

"You said we could go to the ocean, Will."

"I don't know. Are you feeling ... okay?"

She leaned her head against the window.

"Whatever," she said. "Let's just go home."

WE STOPPED THAT night in a small town north of Atlanta. The signs off the highway advertised the local petting zoo with faded photos of peacocks. Alice pointed at them.

"Hey," Alice said. She poked me in the arm. A bit of electricity shocked my skin. "Do you remember the peacocks?" she asked.

"Sure," I said. The first site we'd worked on together had been in a grassy field adjacent to a peacock farm. We'd slept in thin canvas tents, so we heard the birds when they cried in the night. They sounded like children afraid of the dark. Alice and I were grateful for the birds, believing they provided cover for our own nightly noise. When a tornado tore through the site late in the summer, it stripped the birds of their feathers and littered the field with their bodies.

"We never saw any of them alive," she said.

WE WERE IN Indiana again when we ran into a whiteout. The cars slowed to a crawl and then eventually we stopped altogether. I put my blinkers on, but there was nothing to see outside. It felt as if we were in a tunnel, a wormhole, like maybe if I closed my eyes and opened them minutes or hours or years later I might wake to another world. I tried this, staring hungrily at the backs of my eyelids, but when I opened them the world outside was still white and without dimensions and Alice was bouncing her leg and watching me with wide eyes. The headlights from the southbound lane were soft orbs suspended in snowfall. Some people turned their lights off and on, off and on. What were they trying to say? We waited and it snowed in gusts that began to bury the car.

The engine blew cold air through the heat vents and I smelled something on fire. There was a gash of white light in the air that opened up the storm, seemed to split the whole thing at its seam, and for a second I could see the line of cars stopped on the highway ahead, and then the storm closed around us again.

"Thundersnow," Alice said.

Tess started screaming. There was another flash of lightning and the world went harsh white.

"I went to the clinic," Alice said. "I never told you."

"What happened?"

"There was a girl outside, denim skirt to her ankles, waist-length braid, you know. She gave me a hundred-dollar bill and said I could keep it if I didn't go inside."

Alice shivered and I turned to dig in the back, pushing aside the bones and our luggage for a blanket, which I put over her. She looked pale. The snow kept on and on.

"What did you do?"

"I kept the money."

"It's okay," I said.

"I hope we die," Alice said. Her eyes were closed.

"You don't mean that."

But I couldn't be sure. Tess screamed louder and neither of us reached for her. It seemed all our time since she was born could be divided into two existences—the one in which Tess slept and the one in which she screamed.

"I do. I've lost it."

A white, hot fear spread out from my heart.

"Stop," I said.

"You're not listening. You never listen to me."

She unbuckled her seat belt and the car shuddered in the wind. She twisted her body around and reached for Tess. I was afraid of her. She held our baby tight to her breasts and Tess quieted for a minute, rooting for the nipple, but when Alice didn't pull her shirt down, Tess started screaming again.

"For Christ's sake, Alice, just feed her already."

But she wouldn't. Instead she took the palm of her hand and put it over Tess's tiny face, covering her nose and mouth, and she went silent without her breath, and I slapped Alice hard on the face, waking her from herself, maybe, and when her arms went slack I took Tess and held her into my sternum, where she still searched for Alice's nipple. I kissed Tess's eyelids, which were squeezed shut. Tried to think of something to say. Alice unbuttoned her shirt and her breasts were red, inflamed. She held her hands out and I wanted to keep Tess; I didn't trust Alice at all, but I knew the baby was hungry and I couldn't help her. I handed her over to Alice.

Tess was finally dozing when I heard the sirens moving toward us. It was dark and massive drifts of snow continued to blow over the car. I thought I could see headlights, but maybe I was delirious. I couldn't feel my feet. I tried the door but it was jammed, and guessing by the windows I figured the drift was four or five feet high. It was still snowing, although the wind seemed to be dying down. The sirens were closer and there was the sound of plows, the scrape of shovels, the swinging beams of flashlights. There were four National Guardsmen with headlamps and they pried the driver's door open. One of them leaned in and his lamp lit up the inside of the car so brightly I squinted.

The guardsman started to help me out, but I stopped him when I remembered the bones. The skeleton in the trunk was a lost cause, but I grabbed the box in the back seat, the one containing the juvenile remains, and held it to my chest as he pulled me out of the car by my armpits and I scrambled up through the tunnel of snow and into the night. On top of the drift, I sank a couple of inches and saw the car was buried much deeper on the other side; the snow had blown high over the top of the passenger door. The stretch of highway ahead was tundra. As far as I could see tiny armies were digging people out. I held the box tightly, suddenly petrified of spilling the bones on the highway, losing them for good.

I crouched down to see Alice coming up out of that snow tunnel with Tess zipped into her coat. The guardsman was already up and out; she'd probably refused the help I'd accepted from him. She came out from the snow cave looking like some picture from my

Anthro 101 textbook—an erotic portrait of an early human, wild hair, eyes shining, a child strapped to chest.

The guardsmen escorted us to the tanks, and then to a motel in town.

IT WAS AN old one-story motel—a wraparound building with white plastic chairs outside, doors that opened right onto the parking lot. A man was smoking a cigarette outside his room, wearing sweatpants tucked into snow boots. In the strip mall across the parking lot, I bought two bottles of red wine and Chinese takeout. I sat on the edge of the bed and ate out of the cartons. Tess slept in the hotel crib. There was a TV on the dresser and a mirror on the bathroom door that faced the bed. Looked as if there were fingerprints on it, like maybe somebody had fucked against it, or else someone had touched her mirror self with greasy hands, once. Alice took a shower and then sat down with me. She put her head in her hands and the vertebrae in her neck were sharp knobs. I thought of the box of bones I'd left buried beneath the snow. Alice toyed with a fortune cookie. She rolled the paper between her fingers and I remembered her hand over Tess's face in the car.

"The doctor gave me something," I said.

She rolled her eyes. "He gave me the pamphlets, too, Will."

"Maybe when we're back in Milwaukee we should see about getting you some help."

It wasn't what I'd wanted to say.

"You think I'm crazy," she whispered.

"No, baby, no."

"Of course you do."

She pushed me back on the bed and her towel fell away. She took off all my clothes and kissed me so her tongue touched my tonsils.

"This is it, right?"

I wanted to say no, no, it's not, but it would have been a lie and when I smelled the place behind her ear I was so hard I said nothing at all. It had been months. She worked her tongue all the way down my chest and stomach and when she took my dick in her mouth, I wanted badly to be inside her or at least to touch her or smell her, but she stayed down there with her hips over my knees and one hand on my balls until I almost came, and then she bit down on me and I cried out and flipped her onto her back. I drove myself down into her throat, and I knew she couldn't breathe, and I put my hand on her neck and felt myself there, and when I came she reached up and put her fingers in my mouth and pulled me down to her, and I kissed her so I tasted myself, and I licked her lips for her. I tried to touch her, to open her legs gently, but she swatted me away and closed her eyes. I fell asleep fast.

I woke to a cry that did not belong to Tess. The door to the bathroom was open just a crack, and a slice of harsh fluorescence shone onto the bed and my body. I got up and watched Alice through the crack, one leg up on the sink, her back curved, her feet arched, one hand between her legs. I pushed the door open and she sank down onto both feet and turned toward me.

"What are you doing?"

Her face was flushed; she was still naked, her hair hanging around her shoulders. I imagined putting my hands in it. Maybe I wanted more. Maybe I wanted too much. I went to her. She put her hand up to stop me.

"I want to make you come," I told her.

"I can't."

"Please."

She lifted herself up and sat on the edge of the sink. And I went to her, put one hand behind her head and touched the insides of her thighs with the back of the other. I got down on my knees and pushed her legs apart. Her vagina was still split with a dilapidated railroad of black stitches: the places where the dissolving threads had gone in and out of the skin were red and white and sticky with something that didn't smell like her at all. I turned away, and hated myself for it.

She grabbed my head and pulled it back, pointed at the stretch of stitches still left, a second angry mouth, and said, "You did this to me."

———————

Willa C. Richards is a graduate of the Iowa Writers' Workshop, where she was a Truman Capote Fellow. Her debut novel, *The Comfort of Monsters*, is forthcoming with Harper (2021).

EDITOR'S NOTE

When I think about what it means for *The Rumpus* to be a home for "stories that build bridges, tear down walls, and speak to power," I think of Kristen Sahaana Surya's "Gauri Kalyanam." Surya weaves a tale that feels timeless and timely, foreign and familiar, artful and effortless all at once. From its first sentence—"Her heartbeat is a history folded into a vessel."—"Gauri Kalyanam" engages readers with its beautiful language and exquisite storytelling. Rather than moralizing or preaching, Surya utilizes craft and story to impart important, universal truths about gender inequality and patriarchy.

Kristen Sahaana Surya's poetic voice sings on the page, and I'm thrilled this artful, wise story will be celebrated as a PEN America/Robert J. Dau Short Story Prize winner. I have no doubt that Surya is an emerging talent to be reckoned with, and we're proud to have given her first published piece a home at *The Rumpus*.

Marisa Siegel, Editor in Chief
The Rumpus

GAURI KALYANAM

Kristen Sahaana Surya

HER HEARTBEAT IS a history folded into a vessel. When she is born her mother counts three beats where two should sound: an arrhythmic omen embedded in a baby's chest. She is born black, not brown, and on her first full moon she is offered the sweet-sounding titles of fair-skinned goddesses. Her mother smells her skin in kisses and calls to her: Papa, my Papa, Chinna Papa, Kutty Papa, my darling baby girl. When she is still small her mother rubs her with turmeric powder and coconut oil, callused hands stroking soft skin, until her body buzzes with the softness and the brightness of a woman whose existence depends on erasure. Her mother's hands snap chicken necks, pound rice, and pull her hair. Her mother's hands hold the cash that comes in her dowry, tie the collar of the cow in their yard, and slap her face a thousand times to rid it of its ugliness. Her mother's hands are bilingual: to her face, which they seize and smack and spit, they are hammers against nails; but to her hair, which they comb and braid softly before bed, they are the amma whose eyes refuse to meet her own.

She is sold to a man twelve years her senior.

She is sold with the promise of cash and a cow.

On the day of her wedding her heart beats twice.

———

HER HUSBAND IS called Vasu and he carries the face of a bull. He is wider than she expects, but also taller, and a gash sits square in the seat of his chin. A round ring of plated gold hangs from the sliver of flesh between his nostrils. Red, infected, and oozing, it clanks against her teeth as he pushes into her hips at night. He does not drink or smoke or gamble. He does not wash his mouth or clean his teeth or kiss her in the dark.

She spends her days reading filmi magazines that she pulls from the next-door neighbor's trash. In the evenings, she prepares dishes she knows he will eat without complaint. When he relishes a meal, he eats in thick silence marred only by the steady smacking of his lips. When the food does not suit his taste, he asks her where she learned her cooking, and laughs before she can answer.

"I knew you were a good woman when your father told me you stopped school in the third standard," he says often. "Good women learn when to stop learning."

Before the monsoons they go to the movies. He takes her to see *Singari* at the theater behind their house one night, where he buys red-buttered masala popcorn and holds her limp fingers in his wide hand.

"Padmini is the greatest actress of our time," she tells him as they sit, "but you can still hear her accent when she speaks Tamil."

"Too many movies will make you lazy," he says.

She does not take any of his popcorn.

When the movie is over, he takes her to a newsstand outside the theater and points to a magazine with Padmini's face.

"If I buy you this," he asks, lilting his voice toward her with the promise of affection, "will you enjoy the pictures?"

She takes it from his hand and pretends she cannot read the title.

But he is sweet sometimes, too, sweet-speaking and eyes dancing with yearning looks. His house is her first home without a mother, and in the night when she uncoils her hair, it is he who sits behind her with a comb, murmuring soft stories in her ears as he layers her hair in threes. He pins her plait with fresh flowers and inhales near her neck as if he is making a memory.

When life swells in her belly she dreams of Yashoda. She envisions peacock-blue babies born with the power to suckle the breasts of demons. She dreams of a son born to strangle snakes made of men, of a daughter born to stamp the earth open and accept a woman whole into its womb. The midwife comes and she spreads her legs and pushes pain into personhood.

Her son is born black, not blue, and when he wails he is handed to her, bloody sac streaming and white cord uncut. She holds her boy in her elbow and studies the wholeness of him. Two arms, two legs, black hair, one mother. She runs her finger against his gums and sees the whole world sitting in the center of his mouth. There it all sits: blue sea and sky, green earth and soil, fabled myth and man, swirled into a globe at the base of his throat. How vast it was, the whole wide world around them: hung idly between teeth and tongue, caught or carefully kept in the crevices of a toddler's gums.

HERE IS THE history she cannot ignore: her first tooth fell when Vasu began to hit her.

First on the back of her neck, so that no one would see, and then, next, when the sights and sounds of her battered body could no longer bother him, her face, and then the cigarettes, whose burns trailed the length of her arms like a lover's lost kisses. Papa, *Baby*, he called her, like everyone else, but she found herself hunching tightly over their children—two sons, now—as they suckled her breasts, as if she were a wall. Not soft or pink or sweet, like the gums his fists had left behind, but a solid steel tooth in her own right. Twenty-three years young: toothless, fearless Papa.

He himself is not fearless, and when the walls within her rise she watches his hurricane melt. He runs his thumbs across her cheekbones. He begs to hold her child.

She studies her sons for signs of the bull within them. When they are still small, her mother tells her, they will crawl and hit and hurt each other. This is the male nature, to hurt, but you are their amma and you will soften them with your woman ways.

But they are bubbly balloons, colorful fat candies stuffed with laughter and sweetness and good-smelling hair. She cuddles them close and covers her bruises. She runs her finger across their tiny teeth at night, covering them with fluoride and sweet dreams. Vasu buys them gold chains and used books and bright colored balls. When their eyes grow wide with fear, he hides his fists, sets them into his pockets until she is in the bath or the bedroom, until they are alone and the children are sleeping. He pounds her face into dry cement. She does not scream. Her eyes search the drawer of her dowry.

She begins to count the cash she came with.

"HER NAME IS Madhavi," Vasu says.

Madhavi stands behind her husband in the doorway. She is

small and black-haired and red-eyed, and when Papa speaks she looks at her feet.

"Yes, that's all fine," she says. "Who is she?"

Vasu holds Madhavi's hand in his and brings her to his left side and says, "She is my wife. She is to be my wife."

"And who am I?" Papa asks him.

"You are my first wife," he says, reaching his right hand toward her. "You are a good woman and my first wife and you will learn to love Madhavi as I have learned to love you."

"And who am I?" she asks him again. "Who do you think I am?"

.

DEPARTURE LOSES ITS question mark. Satchel bags quickly stuffed with coins and cash, babies clinging to her neck, she flies into the warm night, the sounds of Vasu's snores trailing behind her.

After they leave him they find a yellowed straw hut. They are lucky to have it, yes, because while the hut itself is barely a hut, thatched roof and tarp door, they are still together: Baby and her babies, cooking chicken on an open flame and waiting in paranoid peace for him to come and collect.

Her eldest watches her while she sleeps. She feels his eyes boring into the bony shoulder under her sari. He is a young man, nearly six years old, and soon she will have to buy clothes for him. His penis protrudes when he walks, strutting around the house like a rooster claiming his roost.

"If he comes here," her son tells her, "if he comes here, let me handle things."

His brother is too young for him to hold, but he is still the man of the hut and the least she can do is to let him think it.

She wonders what work can be done with her body. The women in the huts adjacent see her scars and slip her cash; when she refuses, they call their boss.

"We can't sell sex without teeth," he declares, "but her legs are firm and we need laborers."

In the mornings, the lady laborers tie cotton cloths around the width of their heads to better balance beams and bricks against their skulls. The beams are heavy stone and Papa cannot lift them with her arms alone, but she holds them high against her towel, slipping slightly in the wobble of her chin and the shake of her shin against her babies' pulling palms. She is paid twelve rupees a day for her service, or so she is told—she does not count the cash.

Men wander from hut to hut during the dusty break hour, searching for food and conversation and company. She is grateful for the screaming children, for the bright toothless smile she must offer them.

"Amma," the men call her, an unfamiliar ring of respect denting their hoarse voices, "Mother, thanks for the meal."

They bring her rice, squirreled or stolen from somewhere, and bright pull toys for the children. They address her eldest as a man. They leave her clothes untouched.

In the evenings, she squats in circles with the beam balancers and the hut dwellers, slapping wet turmeric into each other's skin to stop the darkening. There is a cool feeling against her dry joints and a warm feeling in her chest. The younger girls have a secret hope of lightening their complexion, and she tells them again and again and again that it will work, that there will be a handsome hero at the end of the film, that bright skin and a sweet smile will somehow send them soaring.

The house that she is building has eight bedrooms and a veranda.

She studies the blueprints with the wary, wishing eyes of a woman whose hopes have never been granted.

"I will have a house like this one day," she says to the other women, as if it is a joke.

"You and what husband, Papa?" they ask her. "Who will buy this house for you?"

"I will buy two," she says.

The palm who pays her grabs her wrist. It is the forceful grab of a startled man who has only just been bothered, or the desperate grab of a man who has only just begun wanting.

She clangs her coins against his jaw, silver clashing against his small white teeth. She pushes his face away with her open palm. Her stomach is clenching. She tells him to let go, or perhaps she does not—she cannot hear herself over the thick cloud of her fear.

The scars on her arm bore holes into his eyes. His face carries the freshly stung sadness of disappointment, and she sees that he is staring at the burns on her arm, at the scars on her shoulder, at the pinkness of her smile.

"I am sorry," he says, eyeing the children clinging to her sari.

"I am not," she tells him.

He opens his wallet. "Take something."

She shakes her head. "Work, yes. Not money. Not money only."

He narrows his eyes as he thinks. "Housework?" he asks. "My wife needs help at home."

She asks how many bricks she will have to carry.

"No bricks," he promises, "only babies, Papamma."

And then she is Baby and Mother together, past and present welded to one.

———

THE PAYROLL OFFICER lives in Adyar, one hour from the hut by
public transit bus, so she straps the children to her back and to
her front. They climb aboard, bodies packed tight in stinking heat
and sweat, unwashed men gazing at the small curve of her breasts.
Their dark faces flicker into Vasu's—the bright gold of his ring
sinking out of their nostrils—but when she smiles at them, toothless and leering, she sees their faces flinching and feels freedom
flying in her belly.

The children she cares for are sullen and stubborn, ignoring her
sons and her endless offers to prepare sweets.

"Tell us a story," they demand, and when she has run the reams
of births and deaths dry, has told every trial of every god, she asks
if they have yet heard the story of Devadasu and Parvati.

"No?" she asks, etching incredulity into the curves of her
mouth. "First," she says, "think of a dark theater, and when the
screen turns light, Savitri is sitting in the royal court . . ."

There are months. Papamma makes magic out of movies and
feels tension building in her belly. She hears from a cousin of their
old neighbor that Vasu is searching, that he is angry, that he wants
his children.

"Keep them close, Papamma" the women whisper. "He can find
you with his eyes closed."

She sees him slipping through the doors of huts in the deep black
of night, and balancing beams across his head with the women in
the mornings. She sees him selling fruit and milking cows, teaching
maths to her children, and stitching saris at the tailor. She sees him
married to Madhavi and tied, too, to the hundreds of women in the
huts who look like her.

"Rest easy," her neighbors tell her, "if he comes here, he will
have to come through us."

Her sons wrestle with sleep, bulls charging through their dreams, and in the dark dank of the hut she cannot soothe them.

"He will come to the school," she warns them when they wake. "He will try to give you money, he will try to take you away." Do not leave me, she thinks, but she does not say it, because it cannot leave her lips and it does not need to be spoken.

When he comes for her, he is quiet and final.

He waits at the bus stop in Adyar. His shirt is full of soot and his hair is caked with dust.

"How did you find me?" she asks. "How did you come here?"

"What's one neighborhood," he says, "what's two when there is love at the other end?" His voice is freshly churned butter hanging high on a pot. "Come home," he asks her. The weight of the question is caught between them.

"Home is not your house."

"Madhavi misses you," he says, in the wheedling way of yearning for truth in his own lies. "I miss our sons, and she misses her sister."

"Sister?" she says. "Leave me. Leave my children be. Leave me, leave me."

"You will come," he insists, and he reaches for her arm.

She feels the softness above the bones in his hard palm.

Then there is the bus and the door, and she is hiding in the thickets of men until the back of his sooty white shirt fades into the swarms of workers at the station. She clutches the window frame, catching her breath and feeling her pulse. The bus pulls forward.

STACKS OF CASH grow taller than her sons. She sews her savings into the hems of her petticoats, and when they weigh her down, she buys thick gold belts that she fastens across her broad belly. At night her eyes close and grow green: she converts belts to houses, belts to bedrooms, belts to Western toilets and marble verandas. Belts become private schools and eggs at every meal. Belts become doctor visits and clean teeth. Belts trace the shape of her waist and the length of her life, and when she feels them move under her sari she feels a deep-set satisfaction.

She visits a newsstand and pays for a filmi magazine to read at teatime.

"I saw you here with your husband once," the vendor says, and she shakes her head, belts clanging beneath her blouse.

"You saw some other woman," she says.

The vendor studies the brightness of her blouse and nods. "You may be right," he says. "Anyway—that man passed some months ago."

WHEN THE GODDESS called Savitri chased Yama to the ends of the earth, for a dead husband whose life was not yet finished, she charmed Death with her words and fooled him with her wisdom. Papamma thinks of Savitri Devi, that cunning mother goddess and her white-willed tongue, and then—sticky-smiled—of the wide-eyed Savitri Ramasamy, whose Bollywood business was plastered on the front of every new magazine she purchased. The actress's husband was a liar and cheat, the rumors said; famous actor and all that, and still a man with two women.

There will be a pyre, she is told, and she is alight briefly with the thought of Vasu's body burning, but she cannot bring herself to watch him melt to black ash. She shaves her head and burns her bright clothes. Her sons swaddle her shoulders in gray-brown cloth and she clutches them close to her dry red eyes.

"For him?" they ask her. "Still, for him?"

"A marriage is a marriage," she says.

Madhavi comes to the hut.

Her heart beats in threes. She does not answer the door.

Kristen Sahaana Surya is a student of fiction at the Program for Writers at Warren Wilson College. She is a lawyer living in New York City.

EDITORS' NOTE

From the first sentence, Sena Moon's story grabbed our attention. There's something so deliciously strange and alluring about this story's syntax that makes everything feel a little off-kilter. A deep and treacherous darkness looms beneath every surface of this story—in the vivid descriptions of Seoul, and what at first seems like a mundane conversation between two former friends. Moon crafts conversation with such skill and unravels the dark underbelly of her characters' lives to create a wholly surprising and compelling narrative.

Michelle Donahue, Prose Editor

Alyssa Greene, Prose Editor

Quarterly West

DOG DREAMS

Sena Moon

"Hello, hello," goes the voice, immediate and rushed. It gives me an unexpected long pause to decide whether to hang up on this intrusion. Just when my thumb decides yes, I hear the voice calling out, "Jimin-ah, is that you?" before drowning into nothingness. My thumb perspires against the heat of the END button. It's Yeju.

Seoul is sweltering that summer. Sometime around May, the sun became a nuisance and not a sporadic beacon of warmth and beauty. By June, hellfire. People share near-death experiences over the phone and I secretly rejoice. The heat wave is as good a reason as any to remain in status quo, holed up and hunched in my room, festering.

"Please don't call again," I write back. "Even with a different number."

But my phone pleads. "An hour," it says, "just an hour. Okay, thirty minutes. Even less. Please."

We meet at a tent bar where older men drink alone. The orange tent is partially open to let out the heat. A rickety fan spews hot air in the corner, facing the cook, whose face is awash in an oily red sheen that resembles the color of her apron. We order food. The smell of scallions sizzling in fresh oil makes heads turn lazily toward the sky, whiffing and panting.

"I'm paying." Yeju scrambles over to the counter. The cook palms the money and offers us soju in return. Silently, we each down a shot and watch the flour puddles turn golden brown on the skillet.

Yeju is barefaced today, her formfitting blouse a smattering of funfetti against white polyester. The flimsy material is sticking to her skin and turning beige. Below, a pencil skirt of moderate length, no heels. A cheap vinyl bag with the print of a running poodle on its side completes the look. Not her usual form. In fact, it looks more my speed. I could have worn that skirt.

She catches me assessing.

"How've you been doing?" she asks.

I've been telling close acquaintances I've been sick. "Benign tumor. That threatens to be aggressive."

The cook scissors thick pancakes into manageable portions before serving them up. The sides are burnt and crispy, a little too much flour and not nearly enough scallion. Yeju tears off the burnt bits before she wolfs down a piece.

"So," I prompt. "Start talking."

The hollow of her cheek bulges as she pushes her mouthful to the side, chipmunk-like. She begins.

It all started with a man and ended with his wife slapping her in front of six of her coworkers. The man, K, had a small apartment and a Hyundai Avante to his name, and also a funnel chest that prevented him from getting fully nude with her, ever. But he'd shown himself to his wife, and that niggled Yeju.

"I've heard this a million times before," I tell her. "Twenty minutes."

"There's more this time. I promise." She rips into another pancake.

The married K was good friends with another man, an insurance salesman called S. Yeju considered S a proper gentleman because he bought her two glasses of white wine and nothing more. He didn't press for sex. Her sob story to him about being the office wife turned into a nuzzle, where he kneaded her thighs with his veiny hands as he gently headbutted her neck over and over again. One night, he drove her along Han Kang Bridge and they watched the rainbow lights "flirt with the night sky"—his words.

"I'm leaving," I tell her. I wish to curl up in bed and wake up in December.

"No, listen." Yeju fills her paper cup to the brim. "Initially, I was trying to get back at K; I admit this. But I ended up really digging S. I met his family and all."

She drums her fingers on her neckline. "S had a brother. Slim, good-looking kid, only seventeen. He was a neujdung-i, thus the absolute baby of the family. The mother was forty-six when he was born."

The man next to us snorts. Yeju ignores him or, rather, doesn't notice.

"His brother was blind. Nothing congenital. This kid was born healthy and stayed in tip-top condition throughout his adolescence. Then he suddenly went blind when he was sixteen."

Her hand makes a pulling motion as if she's switching off a light. Despite myself, I am hooked. Yeju has a knack for this, which is why she was so successful as a bar hostess. Most girls there just listened, but Yeju could really talk.

"Naturally the family was devastated, S most of all. He adored his brother, from what I've heard. In fact, he claims he's only ever loved me like he loves his little brother."

I gag. "It's a sales pitch. He's in insurance."

"Right. But the insurance payout saved his family. They were about to lose the house. The mother was diabetic, which led to renal insufficiency, which eventually led to hospice care. The father lost his job in a layoff and refuses to wash himself anymore, because what's the point? Add to that the poor blind boy and you've got yourself a chronic *situation*"—she uses the English word—"and S felt guilty because he thought, well, blood money. That money saved them."

Yeju takes a pause to swig and I follow suit.

"They say soju tastes sweet when you're miserable," she titters nervously.

I'm entirely unimpressed with this role she's given herself. "And?"

"And, well. He decided anyone he cared about should understand the benefits of insurance. You never know when you might drive your car off the road or go blind."

"That's awful pessimistic of him."

"Like you, Jimin. Your semi-benign tumor?" She challenges me now, her heavy-lidded, half-moon eyes waxing. I am waiting for the moment she asks me to partake in her beau's insurance scheme.

"Anyhow, I told S the only way I'd spring for a policy that big is if he'd do it with me. And like I told you, he's a gentleman. He applied first. I applied next. We are moving toward a new level of commitment as a couple."

"How stupid are you?" I ask.

"No, but we are."

She plucks a ring from the depths of her blouse, tethered to her neck by a delicate silver chain. Baby diamonds huddle in a neat line atop a thin platinum road. The ring looks a hair too small for her fingers and does not belong in this seedy tent. "He proposed," she says.

"Did he?" My plastic stool scrapes concrete as I stand. The alcohol shoots to my brain and my teeth start to pound. "This was mildly interesting."

"Jimin-ah."

"Good to see you, Yeju. I think we're done here."

I walk through the tent flaps without saying goodbye, realizing a few drunken steps later I've left my sandals under my seat.

Yeju emerges a moment later in a halo of light, my sandals in one hand and her vinyl bag smothering her chest in the other. Her mouth rounds into an O as she trips over a beveled tile on the sidewalk, releasing a scratchy yelp as she lands on hard concrete. On all fours, she looks up and addresses the night sky. "I'm fine."

I quicken my pace. Yeju tails me. Gravel bites into the soles of my feet as Dangsan Road expands and brightens upon itself, and I reach the four-way intersection where two boys and a girl are walking a Pomeranian dressed in red booties. This nugget of a dog gets critical of my dirty, naked feet and proceeds to wrap its strap around me as it loop the loops, *yip-yip-yip.*

"Ottokhe—I'm so sorry." The girl apologizes as she hands the harness to her friends and helps me loose. Twenty yards back, Yeju is still hobbling after me with shredded knees. When the streetlight hits her squarely, all three adolescents gasp and jaywalk from the site, dog in arms. The light turns blue.

Yeju finally catches up and throws herself onto my back. Her arms snake over my clavicles as my back arches, my legs kicking up seconds after my brain tells them to, slow and heavy like they belong to someone else. My mouth is smashed against her biceps.

MAC Ruby Woo lipstick drags along the polyester, leaving permanent garish streaks. There is no one around, only cars.

"His little brother didn't go blind," Yeju gasps. "S took out a
youth insurance policy a year before that kid went blind."

I go limp.

"From a syringe." Her arm is a hot noose, her whisper scallions
and liquor. "He said the needle went in like going through thick
pudding. Or like yanggaeng, red bean bars. S was crying buckets
when he told me."

Sensing my body slacken, she unfolds herself some.

"Would you listen now?"

I nod. We are face-to-face. Yeju gives me a look I instantly
recognize as the one from my wedding, the time she caught the
bouquet.

She was my purse gal. Yeju flanked me throughout the pre-
ceremony, collecting envelopes stuffed with cash and holding my
purse while suits and mid-length dresses floated into the boudoir
and took glossy photos of us looking unnaturally happy. My parents didn't approve of this harlot, this semi-prostitute-in-waiting—
as my mother called her—standing in as my best girl. My mother,
the stay-at-home tutor, and my father, a distinguished professor
of a university no one has ever heard of—they like to think themselves as proper, well-meaning folk. They did little to hide their
contempt. Yeju stayed until the end, her beautiful nails a bloody
mess by mid-reception from being chewed on when she thought no
one was looking.

I should've defended her. But her social accounts are peppered
with documentation of takeout coffees and beautiful food, men
with missing heads that only hint at the identity of the recorded.

The most they show are pearly smiles, because Yeju crops every photo she uploads to keep her life undefined.

Yet defined her life was, at least in my eyes. She used to tell me stories about her men, paying clients and nonpaying ones. The way her hair cascaded onto pillows of every bachelor pad and motel imaginable—once, the back seat of a moving train; once, the gleaming wooden surface of a temple floor. The smell of hand sanitizer. Sanitized hands patting under pillows, groping for a condom, a knife, an ulterior motive, for her phone, to tell me that I was the only person she could truly be open with ever since that day we met in the hospital where we both lost something: her a womb and me a baby. In the end, her stories meld together—the motels, card keys, and cheap toothbrushes that spit bristles into her mouth so that she eventually gives up and gargles using her own travel-size Listerine, spitting again and again into a bowl that is perpetually coated with fluid, under a light that casts violet shadows on her face. I may have tolerated my mother's vision of Yeju, if not outright believed it.

She didn't want the bouquet. I threw it to her anyway. When the time came, she caught the flowers half-heartedly, almost quizzically, as if the hydrangeas and peonies had taken flight by their own volition and landed in her arms, like an evil omen, or a reminder. When we locked eyes amid the flurry of cheers, Yeju shot me a look. Later, before I went off to Saipan for my honeymoon, she toasted me and slurred: *Be happy enough for the both of us.*

"I'm planning to do the same to K," the Yeju in front of me says.

"What?"

We are still under the streetlights, backed by the constant flow of traffic. I look down and half expect to see my wedding dress dragging in hot gravel.

"You're the only person I'm telling." She pats the rump of her vinyl bag. "K took out an insurance policy, too, under S's guidance."

"Are you still seeing K?"

"No." She shakes her damp curls. "Could if I wanted to."

"Did S put you up to this?" I ask, feeling more absurd by the minute. "How do you know S won't do the same to you? After all, he blinded his own brother."

She considers. "I just know," she says. "That brother is living with us now. We're paying for his everything, and that's okay. I'm living with S, and that's okay, too."

I watch Yeju rummaging around in her bag, fishing for validation.

"If anyone finds out," she says, "I'm going to bring this to the authorities." The syringe rests at the bottom of a ziplock bag. "He kept it," she says.

We walk back together. Our tired legs glide over the intersection, the flickering lights, the tent bar, the gravel. We are swept into the maw of a dark building, lifted by an elevator that smells vaguely of dead roses, cat pee. At the entrance of my apartment, Yeju leans tentatively against the doorway, tracing her breath with palms folded over her chest.

"We're friends, aren't we?" she asks.

"Maybe." I wave her off. "I might tell on you."

"That's a chance I'm willing to take."

Yeju sinks gently to the floor, shivering despite the heat. A paper-thin rivulet of blood is traveling down her left shin, heading straight for the talus. She says she's not drunk, just exhausted.

As she lies still on the sofa, her head slowly dividing the two cushions propped beneath her cranium, I dress her wounds with Mercurochrome, dabbing red over red.

"What did it look like?" she suddenly asks.

"What?"

"His chest. I want to know." Her eyes are wide open, thick pudding and red bean bars.

"Search up any old funnel chest on the web and you'll see."

Yeju shakes her head. "But it's not his, y'know. I just want to know what was so bad about it that he had to hide the damn thing."

The deep hollow of K's chest floats by my line of vision, a fleshy bowl that cradled my palm every night for the six years we've been married. He cried real tears the day he revealed it to me. He cried over many things, one pearly tear for each flaw.

"With no kids in the picture, you're going to get a good amount." Yeju smiles. "Maybe you can go back to school. Or try flying yoga. Remember you wanted to try flying yoga?"

I don't remember a time when I wished for such things. Yeju dozes off, her nose kissing the hash-mark surface of my sofa. Her handbag is half open and loose by my feet. Her knees are an open wound, as are my soles, and I vaguely recall my high school teacher saying, *Heat travels up, girls, heat travels up.* My body burns as I drift into an adjacent room, dialing.

K picks up and calls out my name, then "Hello, hello," immediate and rushed. "Jimin-ah, is that you?" He's ready to come back home.

I open my mouth to find a blister taking over, knotting gray matter over my failing lips, sealing them shut.

———————

Sena Moon is a graduate of the MFA program in prose at University of Michigan's Helen Zell Writers' Program, where she was a recipient of the Tyson Award in Fiction and the Hopwood Undergraduate Short Fiction Award. She is the third-place winner of *Glimmer Train*'s Short-Story Award for New Writers (May/June 2018). She hails from Seoul, Korea.

EDITOR'S NOTE

"Bat Outta Hell" is masterful at peering into a family—a whole world—from the point of view of a character who is as much a part of that world as apart from it. We know little of Julian's motivations, and somehow that limited— may we say hazy—perspective tells us everything. There is no aha moment in the grappling of sexuality, no meditation on what it means to be a man, and yet the observations of Julian, the actions of Jay, and the behavior of the peripheral characters all contribute to this family's cosmography. The editors felt this story included all the necessary details to render a vivid and unique portrait, enlivened by a protagonist whom we love, without knowing if he could love us back.

Foglifter was so impressed by Damitri's writing that we recently asked him to join our editorial team as an assistant prose editor.

Miah Jeffra, Co-Founding Editor
Foglifter

BAT OUTTA HELL

Damitri Martinez

THE SOUND OF Jay's new motorcycle found me like a fury. It was faint at first, a storm on the horizon. Then I saw him slingshot around the corner, bringing all that noise with him. He hung a sharp left and revved the bike before he skidded to a stop on the street in front of our house. I was already standing on the sidewalk. I could feel the heat and noise radiating off the bike like a small sun. Jay revved it and everything exploded. Those savage pops and cracks, the metal gurgle of pipe, all of it looped around my lungs, twisted around my gut and groin. It filled me up and rattled me. I wanted to challenge that crazed noise with a primal growl, or throw myself into its hot mechanical core. He revved it again and all the trees and leaves, all the brick bungalows and sidewalks lining the asphalt shimmered, threatening to shake loose their rough surfaces and show us the dark stuff the world was really made of.

"Get that shit off my property!" my grandma yelled from the top of the porch stoop, but we could barely hear her.

My uncle revved the bike again and again to spite her. The more he did it, the more I wanted to try it myself, to twist the handle and release the wild animal of that noise. And then he shut it off.

The silence pushed in on my ears and made me dizzy. All the other sounds on the street hunkered low in the twilight.

Jay unclicked his helmet and pulled it off. He shook his head so his wavy black hair fell to his shoulders. His slender eyebrows were pulled into a scowl. He had high cheekbones and a sharp nose that made him seem meaner than he knew how to be. The few hairs he could grow on his face were trimmed into a neat goatee.

"Jesus Christ," my grandma said. "Stealin bikes now?"

Jay got off the bike in one slick motion and flicked his hair behind his shoulders with a gloved hand. He wore mirrored sunglasses even though the sun was gone.

"I bought it, vieja."

"*Bought* it?" my grandma yelled. "You don't have any fuckin money! What'd you buy it with?"

"None ya," he said, and started rolling the motorcycle down the long driveway to the shed at the back of the house.

I looked up at my grandma on the porch. One of her arms was folded beneath her breasts, the other holding a cigarette expelling tight curls of smoke. Her anger bristled and then turned to ember as she mumbled curses to herself. I followed behind Jay, dragging my Adidas sandals so they wouldn't fall off my feet and the ground wouldn't fuck up my tube socks. I could still feel the wake of heat from the bike on my bare chest.

"Fuckin sick, huh?" he asked me in the shed.

It was a Harley-Davidson, apple red, with a wide leather seat and fringes on the seams. There were two lockboxes on the bike, one in the back and one on the left side, both accented in chrome piping that traced the rest of the frame. The buttons and switches were bright and slick like hard candies. Small chips dotted the arc of the windshield with tiny frowns.

"Who'd you get it from?" We were both stretched out and distorted in the gleam of the chrome. I was Jay's twin in every way, except for the hair. I kept mine buzzed close to my scalp and couldn't grow anything on my face. And I was taller than him by a couple inches.

"None ya." He grinned white teeth at me and then rubbed my stomach because there was no one else in the shed. Then he put the helmet in one of the lockboxes and pulled his hair behind his head with a band. He pulled out a rag from a bin on the shed floor and started rubbing the bike like he was trying to reveal another color underneath all the red. I watched him for a while. Then he got up, turned on the radio to the same rock shit I could hear through our shared wall in the house, took off his leather jacket, and resumed his polishing.

"Get me a beer."

I HAD BEEN living with my grandma and Jay for a year before he got the bike. I was sixteen when I moved in. My mom said it was a temporary thing, me living with my grams in shithole Pueblo, Colorado, while she went to go find work in Cali, but I knew it was bullshit and it eventually turned into the rest of my time in high school, just before I dropped out senior year and moved in with my girlfriend and her brother. Jay was my mom's younger brother, my uncle, but we were so close in age, I dropped the *Tio* when I was twelve and never called him anything but Jay since. He was six years older than me, but my grandma said you wouldn't be able to tell.

"That fuckin mistake. See how he mooches, mi'jo?" She'd be out on her porch, halfway through a twelve-pack of Bud during these confessions, and I'd be out there too, sitting on a ghetto-ass crate right next to her luxury lawn chair. "Coming into my house when he's not shooting up or getting trashed, thinking he owns all this shit."

We would watch the neighborhood come to life, those summer nights. Kids would come flying down the street on those Razors that killed your ankles if you weren't paying attention. Men and women sat in their own chairs on their porches with their beers and cigarettes, the TV flashing through their worn screen doors to empty living rooms. I'd nod my head at other guys I recognized from school or the hangouts Jay took me to. They walked the streets, careful to avoid the orange light pooling from the street lamps.

My grandma was a small puckered woman with a shit ton of wrinkles. She swore it was what years of being out in the sun would do to you, but her brothers would tell you it's because she started sucking Marlboros and dick when she was sixteen and doing it ever since. She worked at the post office and bought a pack of beer after work every Monday. She had bright maroon hair she touched up every month in the kitchen sink, with a dirty hand mirror and the same stained yellow towel draped around her shoulders, like she was some kind of lady to the queen. She drew on her eyebrows with a pencil two shades darker than her hair. She wasn't that old to be a grandmother, something she didn't forget to remind us every chance she got—but sometimes she shuffled around with a hunch and played up all the ailments of a viejita, even though it was probably just a hangover. She always had a cigarette in her right hand and swirled it around while she talked like she was writing everything she said in cursive.

"When I had your mom," she'd tell me in some variation or another, "I told your pendejo grandpa, 'That's it! No more! One's enough!' And ten years later, I almost made it, but then—" She flicked her head back toward Jay's bedroom. "*He* came like a goddamn devil child and cursed my life. Your grandpa died, your moms moved out, and I was left to raise that little shit all on my own." She took another drag and blew out the smoke like a curse. "Don't be him, my sweet Julian," she'd say, flicking her cigarette in my direction.

After a while, Jay would storm out of the house smelling of deodorant and leather, the screen door banging behind him.

"This ain't a hotel!" she'd yell after him, and he'd flip a bird. Before he had the bike, he'd hop into some stranger's car and they'd disappear down the boulevard. But when he got his own wheels, he'd fly down the street "like a goddamn bat outta hell," my grandma would say, and then she'd yell after him, "I'm not payin those bills when you break your goddamn neck!" And she'd suck in more smoke and just for a moment, I'd see all that concern she tried to keep bottled up flare dully like the ash on her cigarette. Then she'd exhale all of it. She started waiting up—*saying* she was waiting for her shows to come on—till she heard the bike come roaring back home.

When I first moved in with my grams, I was an angry little fuck. I missed an entire year of school. I got arrested for tagging the big-ass wall of the community center with some other boys the world forgot. I even called my grams a bitch one night, but she slapped that shit right out of my mouth like a tooth and I spent the night crying from the pain and from the shame, and if I'm being real, from the fear of losing the one person who would deal with me. I pictured being like those fuckers on Grant Street, thrown out of their homes and looking for families in crack pipes and broken syringes. She tamed me right up with that one slap, and since then, I'd do whatever she said, no matter how embarrassing or crazed.

"Hold my purse."

"Hold my hair."

"Go find your goddamned uncle because it's after two a.m."

But after a while, Jay tamed me too.

"This is what I do, whenever I get so fuckin sick of myself," he'd say to me in some stranger's basement, and then he'd take a hit of something and the world would turn purple and pink and gold. He'd live somewhere like a king for a couple hours before I had to drag him home and lay him out on the dirty futon in his room that smelled like weed and cheap cologne.

He did some hard shit. I mostly just got high in my own bedroom, and I'd read or draw, like some fuckin nerd. Harder nights, I'd stare into the popcorn ceiling and listen to Prince from some old albums my moms left me before she ditched, and I'd replay some of the images of her before she left. I had this fear of forgetting her face, that one day when I was grown and out of the house and walking on the street, I'd run into my mom and not even know it was her.

When people asked me about my dad, I pretended that I gave up on that fucker a long time ago, but when I was high, I used to do this stupid game where I'd create memories that weren't even true. Like this one where I'd picture my mom and my dad taking me to McDonald's and they'd let me get a Happy Meal. My dad would ask the lady behind the counter for the other toys we saw in the posters, so I'd have the full collection of Disney action figures. He'd say he'd pay extra, and then he did, and then we'd stay and eat inside the restaurant, which meant that I got to go play in the playground with the slides that used to shock the shit out of me or the ball pit that always smelled like dirty socks.

This was a real memory, or a series of real memories, but in real life, instead of my dad, it was just preteen Jay, already looking grown. But sometimes when I was really high, I could erase Jay and imagine this asshole I never met.

I told Jay about that one night, and he seemed surprised that I remembered those couple of times when he and my moms would take me out on Sundays. He'd look at me, stoned as fuck, and the memory seemed to pull me sharply into his focus.

"That was the only nice thing I ever did for your moms," he'd say, and then he'd take another drag of his cigarette and exhale the memory, tangling it up in the smoke.

My grandma wielded force in that house, but not over Jay. He did whatever he fucking pleased and my grandma seemed to let him. The more Jay pulled me into his shadowy world, the more my grandma seemed to let go of me, no matter how angry she pretended to be with him or me. When she yelled at me for coming home too late with him, instead of anger in her eyes, I'd see this scared and worried look, like a barking dog who knows the thief will come into the house no matter what.

I became a battleground. If my grandma asked me to go to the store with her during the day, Jay would sweep me away and we'd go forget ourselves with some stranger's drugs later that night. I was pulled in both of these directions and we were all waiting to see who would win. But it turned out it wouldn't matter, because soon after, we never saw Jay and his bike again.

THE NIGHT HE brought home the bike, we had to wait until my grams fell asleep before Jay could take me out for a ride.

"Go change your fuckin sandals," he said to me on the porch. I had my sketch pad out and was trying to draw the bike from memory. The street was empty and the sky was the darkest it would be that night. "And put on a T-shirt."

When I came back out, he was holding the sketch pad.

"I want you to design a tattoo for me." He tossed the pad in my direction. "I want that."

I looked down at my rough sketch.

"How long would it take you?"

I shrugged my shoulders. "Not long, if I focused."

Jay disappeared around the house to the shed and then rolled the bike out from the driveway. I waited for him out on the street.

He handed me his helmet.

"You don't have an extra?" I asked.

"We're just goin around the block."

He got on and then I got on, and when he kick-started the motorcycle to life, I felt my balls shoot up into my chest. All that metal felt intent on cleaving my bones apart from my skin, shaking me and shaking me until all that was left was that core part of my body that nobody saw, that part you didn't want anyone to see, not even when you were looking in the mirror. When he kicked off from the asphalt and revved up the speed, I felt like I was riding someone's rage. I clung on to Jay, half expecting to fall over the edge of the world with nothing to grab on to except a fistful of stars.

That night, when we were lying in my bed, he took off his shirt and showed me where he wanted the tattoo.

"Right below el crucifixion."

I stared at his back, which was already half-covered in tangles of dark ink. Roses and brass knuckles took up one shoulder blade and the Virgin Mary took up the other. I looked at the bare spot on his lower back, just beneath the stylized blood drops from the nailed feet of Jesus.

"Touch it, so I know you know where I'm talking about." And I did because I always did what Jay said.

SCHOOL STARTED IN August but my first day wasn't until September that year. I only went to English and art and sometimes after school I'd smoke on the roof with the other girls and boys the world didn't give a shit about. I'd watch the football players down below on the field. They'd turn red with sweat, and then they'd touch each other like they forgot they were guys and I wondered how many of them played football just so they could touch each other without being called a faggot.

The only reason I went to art was that it was the only thing I was kind of good at. And in English, Mr. Diaz was the only teacher who didn't talk down to us. Late in the month we started reading Greek myths. He told us about Zeus and how he had lots of kids with lots of different women and only paid attention to a few. And then he told us bastards that maybe Zeus was one of our dads, and that maybe one of our lazy asses was the next Hercules.

One day I tried to steal a copy of that skinny white book we were reading all the myths from, but Mr. Diaz caught me.

"Now why you stealin somethin you probably woulda gotten for free if you just asked?" he said to me after class. He was tall and dark brown and hard to look at, the way some adults are hard to look at. He always wore a tie and his shirts were never wrinkled. He wasn't mean about what he was asking me. He was smiling.

I couldn't help smiling either since I got caught, but I didn't know what to say, so I shrugged my shoulders and looked away.

"Okay, Closet Reader. Take it. And take these, too." He bent

down to the lowest shelf of the bookcase behind his desk and gave
me two other books. *The Odyssey* and Ovid's *Metamorphoses.*

"Don't steal my shit again." He nodded me out of his classroom.

That night, after I ate the can of refried beans and stale tortilla
chips my grandma bought for dinner, I went to my room at the back
of the house and shut the door. I turned the lock, even though it was
broken, and put a crate of my mom's records in front of the door.
Then I sat on my bed, which was flat on the floor with no frame
or springs, just a bunch of musty pillows and a comforter I hadn't
washed in a couple months, and I pulled out the books Mr. Diaz
gave me. I fished around my nightstand for a joint Jay gave me the
night before, lit it, and then slipped into that lazy space between
reading and thinking. I'd take a drag, read a sentence or a para-
graph, and then fix my attention on something outside my window,
letting the smoke and the words I read twist into new questions or
wonderings. Sometimes I'd write down what came to mind in my
sketchbook, but most nights I just let it all go back up to the stars.

That night I could see the moon from my window. It was halved
like a fruit. The sky took its time turning dark.

I didn't get too far into my ritual before I could hear Jay from the
other side of the wall. There was the music. The mumble of voices.
Then just the music. Then came the dull rhythmic thud of his futon
hitting the space on his side of the wall just above my head.

It was always a puzzle to me who Jay fucked. I never heard or
saw anybody enter or leave the house. I tried to listen one night,
with my ear pressed against the stained wall, but the only voice I
could hear was Jay's low timbre and laugh. It wasn't until one night
I was staring out my window that I saw a hooded shadow slip from
between the house and the tree. He had been using his window and
that made me feel kind of dumb.

Jay and his company finished and I couldn't go back to reading. The book was tented on my chest and the joint was gone. I listened to the sound of Jay's window sliding open and someone landing on the fallen leaves outside the house. A little bit later, Jay came into my room, shoving the crate from the door and knocking it over without picking it up.

"Fuckin nerd. Why you reading?"

He was in a black wifebeater and dirty jeans and was barefoot. His tattooed shoulders were wet with sweat. His hair was greasy and pulled back into a tight ponytail.

He dropped himself at the edge of my bed and grabbed my book.

"*Gods, Men, and Monsters*," he read out loud and then he started to flip through it. "I'm just kidding, you know. Stay in school. Don't be a fuckup."

He tossed the book back to me and rested his elbows on his knees. He tented his fingers in front of his face and tapped them together.

"Want to go out tonight?"

I sat up and put the book on my nightstand on top of his drawing.

"It's Wednesday."

"So?"

"You just told me to stay in school."

He clicked his tongue and wrinkled his mouth to one side as he pulled out his cigarettes from his pocket. He offered me one, but I refused.

"Andre's supposed to have some good shit tonight."

I rubbed my eyes with the palms of my hands. "I'm high as fuck right now," I said.

"Me too," he said, and then he lay back on my thighs. I could feel his head inches from my dick.

After a couple drags, he reached his cigarette-free hand up to my chest and started rubbing me. He would always start with my chest, his fingers stretched and rocking around one pec and then the other. Then he'd work his way down, past the band of my underwear.

"Not tonight, man."

I sat up, displacing his hand. He looked at me and his eyebrows fell over his eyes.

He sucked his teeth and sat up.

"Fuck. You're a real bummer tonight, you know that?"

Then his scowl disappeared and, instead, he looked so tired that it made me want to fall away from him.

Once I heard Jay's bike growl and fade away down the street that night, I tried to return to my book. I opened to a random page and read a story about how one time the Greek version of the devil came up from the ground and stole one of Zeus's daughters, and her mother, who was also Zeus's sister, was so fucked up, she froze the earth and made the first winter, which screwed everyone over. Meanwhile the daughter learned to love the man who stole her and she learned how to become a queen who was supposed to make all the new dead people feel welcomed. The story's main point was supposed to be why we had seasons or some shit like that, but all I could think about was the daughter and how she recognized she felt more at home in hell than she did on earth. And I wondered how much of a choice she actually felt like she had in the matter.

JAY STARTED DOING that shit to me after he caught me doing it to another guy at one of the hangouts he took me to when I first moved in. It was in that guy's basement. There were half a dozen of us there, including a girl called Sam, who Jay had been trying to get me with since I started hanging out with him.

It was a sketchy-ass place with no lights on except for the blue light of a basketball game, the volume turned way down low. The coffee table was trashed with dirty mirrors and bongs, tampers and tongs, like some kind of lazy-ass scientist got too high to finish his experiment. There was a pleather sectional full of limp bodies that shuffled over for Jay to sit and join them. I plopped myself on the floor in a corner, trying to pull myself into something invisible, but the circle of drugs found me and forced me into their dirty circuit of pass-and-smoke. Andre, the host, was on the part of the sectional closest to me. He had on a black bomber jacket with an *A* on the chest, and the same letter scrawled across a black snapback. He kept looking at me like I was going to steal something or rat out what was going on down there. He was holding the hand of his girl, some chick with fat thighs in leopard leggings. The higher he became, the more smiles he sent my way.

I learned quick at those strange parties that you could touch another guy's dick or even blow him, as long as there was a girl who'd do the same to you and as long as nobody saw you doin that shit. And no kissing because kissing meant you were a faggot.

Jay had lots of girls, and I used to think it was them he'd have over to the house without anybody knowing. That night at the hangout, one of them sat on either side of him as he breathed in something from a bowl, opened his arms like wings, and nestled each girl beneath his pits. They laid their ears and dark painted nails on his wifebeater and all three pretended to watch the game. Sam sat on the opposite side of the room from me, the TV light and the smoke making a dense forest we'd get lost in if we tried to meet each other halfway. We blew smoke rings back and forth instead.

I was fucked up on something Andre said was weed but had a tangier taste and left me high two days after. Sometime during the night, while Jay was busy with one of the girls and half the party had left, Andre leaned over to me and caught my hand. He rubbed the back of my wrist with his dark thumb.

"What do you catch with these hands?" he asked, rubbing in concentric circles. And all I could picture in response was a place under the sky where all kinds of stars showered down and kept slipping through my fingers. I couldn't catch a single one.

Jay found us in the bathroom. He pulled me up from the floor and told me it was time to go and I walked home tucked under his arm, like the girls at the party.

I FINISHED SKETCHING Jay's tattoo on an afternoon he and my grandma almost blew the roof off the house. I could hear them through the screen door before I even got up the steps to the porch.

"Why was he here, then?" my grandma shouted at Jay's door. "Tell me. Why. The. Fuck. he was here, then! Open this goddamned door and talk to me like a man!"

I stood in the kitchen with my backpack hanging off my shoulder.

"I told you, if you want to be doin that shit, you better find another goddamned house to do it in!"

I went out the same way I came in and headed for the park just down the block, where I'd wait for the storm to blow over.

The park was small and wound around a dirty puddle of water people called "The Lake." There was a playground for young kids with a slide and a dome of climbing bars that looked like a cage. The whole set was tagged, covered in angular, Sharpied letters. The park was usually trashed because the city was too lazy or too scared to come down and tidy things up on our side of town, but there was one spot under a tree by the overflow ditch where I liked to sit if there weren't any mosquitoes and it wasn't too hot. Sometimes it smelled like piss and stale breath, but I liked that nobody could see you from the park pathway.

But when I got to my tree, I found someone else was already there. Andre was leaning full back into the bark, smoking a cigarette and looking at his phone. He had on his black snapback with the cursive *A* and an oversized T-shirt.

"Julian," he said without getting up. We rubbed hands and pounded fists and he offered me a cigarette. "How's Jay these days?" he asked. "I haven't seen him in a minute."

I shrugged my shoulders. "He's in some shit with my grams right now." I didn't take the cigarette and I didn't sit down.

"Always in some shit." Andre sucked on his cigarette. He held it between his thumb and middle finger, like he forgot how to make an "okay" sign. He laughed. "What kinda shit? You know?"

I shrugged again, readjusted my bag.

"Those are some sweet-ass wheels he got himself. You ride that thing yet?"

I nodded my head and looked up at the park path. A lady with a tattoo on her neck was yelling into her phone. "Yeah. Pretty sweet."

When I looked at Andre again, he was sneering at me. He looked hot and swollen, like if you stuck a stick in him, he'd ooze out something green or gray.

"I'll see you around, man." I turned to go and started walking past the overgrowth of dead grass. It hissed and scratched my shins.

"When you gonna give me that mouth again?"

I stopped and felt the sun hit me in the back of the neck. I turned back to Andre. His hand was on his crotch. "I ain't a faggot, man."

Andre sucked his teeth. "Well, then tell Jay to come suck my dick. I *know* he is."

I walked home and sat on the porch and waited for Jay to rev up his bike and leave for the night. I left my sketch for him on his bed.

A COUPLE DAYS later, Jay showed up at my school during lunch. I heard his bike before I saw it.

"Wanna go for a ride?" he asked without turning off the bike. I saw myself reflected in his sunglasses.

"Sure."

"Helmet's in the back box."

We took the highway toward the mountains. I didn't have a jacket and the higher up we got, the more snot streamed out of my face. Jay finally pulled over at a rest stop that doubled as a scenic overlook.

"Cold as fuck," I said, and I tucked my arms into my T-shirt.

Jay didn't seem to mind the air. We both sat on a bench by the bike. I shivered and he smoked. We sat like that for a while. The sun looked bright and hot but the wind kept swiping away any chance of me feeling it. It didn't help that the trees had already turned into a fire blaze of their own. I thought about my sketchbook and I wanted to go home.

When a cloud covered the sun, I turned around on the bench and surveyed the panorama of empty picnic tables. There were yellow spots in the grass from dog piss. The trash can overflowed with Styrofoam cups and plastic bottles. The parking lot was empty.

Jay finished his cigarette and flicked the butt onto the asphalt.

He stood up and stretched his arms behind him. I got up and leaned over the seat of the bike, resting my chest on my forearms and elbows. The leather seat was warm from the sun.

"Wanna see somethin?" he asked.

Jay unzipped his jacket without waiting for my response. He threw it onto the back of the bike and turned around. He took his wifebeater by opposite ends at his hips and, in one motion, pulled off the shirt.

"Check it out."

There was a square patch of gauze spanning the width of his lower back. Black ink or dry blood dotted the bandage like an inverted constellation.

"Here. Peel it off and take a look."

I came around from the other side of the bike and pulled the tape from two corners and then opened the bandage like a door.

"Whaddya think?"

He'd gotten the motorcycle tattoo.

But it wasn't the one I sketched for him.

This was done by some other artist who probably saw the sketch Jay brought in to him and laughed his head off and then went ahead and drew what was now permanently on Jay's back.

It looked better than anything I could do.

"Did it hurt?" I asked.

"Yeah. Like hell. Took a shit-ton of time, too. Had to go back twice. See the inscription though, at the bottom?"

I peered down at the small of his back, where the skin dimpled above the gray band of his underwear. In scrolling calligraphy were my initials.

My thumb floated over the letters, but I didn't touch him.

"Sick, man." I covered the tattoo with the bandage.

We got back on the highway and I tried my best not to push into the small of his back as we descended the mountain.

THE NIGHT BEFORE Jay disappeared, my grandma threw a football party, like she usually did before the weather got too cold. She'd invite the neighbors and her two brothers and their families. They'd come in their snapbacks and oversized jerseys, twelve-packs and young kids in their tattooed arms. My aunties, the two women married to my grandma's brothers, would be the only ones who'd bring food—chips and deviled eggs and store-bought guacamole and sometimes meat for my grandma's kettle grill, which sat rusting in the backyard. In the purses of the women and in the sagging pockets of the men would be the darker stuff for later, when the game was long over and the teasing and gossip would take a dip.

Everyone would start out watching the game, crammed into my grandma's living room. They'd pass cigarettes and bongs during commercials. The scraps of food on Styrofoam plates would crust over and collect flies. Most of the time for those parties, I'd come out from my room and find a corner to watch. I watched the people more than the game. They sat there on the couches and the armrests and the shag carpet, the smoke slowly weaving them together through the thin lines of light from the TV, pulling them all closer and closer until it seemed like they were one big body with one singular mind, wasted and high as fuck.

Jay wasn't there.

If their team was winning or losing by a lot, the party lost interest and they'd migrate out into the yard if the weather was warm enough. That night was the first night the air started to bite, so all the women stayed inside the house, except for Debbie, my cousin, a dyke who thought she was one of the guys. My uncle Ronnie started the fire pit and all the guys sat around it, drinking cans of Budweiser from a blue cooler that seemed to fill up again every time someone opened it. The kids would run back and forth between the yard and the living room or go to a neighbor's house, lost in their own games, the darkness slowly untethering them from their parents.

After a while, the guy cousins around my age, Debbie included, started getting stupid and smashing empty cans against different parts of their bodies. My cousin Derik upped the ante and poured a drop of the harder liquor into the can, set it on fire with a cigarette lighter and twigs, and then tried to smash the lit can with his foot. We were all supposed to try it, and when I refused, Derik called me a cocksucker. He said it like a curse and I let it do its work on me. I became a specter like the rest of them, violently smashing three cans before realizing I'd scorched my laces. And then I went to sit with the older men, who stared at the fire pit, watching everything from a distance.

The fire lit their faces from below, so the shadows of their noses and wrinkles made them look like hard, worn masks. None of them seemed to see me take a seat in the circle and they kept on their conversation.

"Trudy's too hard on him."

"Trudy ain't hard enough. If he was my son, I'd knock the fuckin shit outta him every chance I got."

"Speakin of, you hear he got his fuckin ass beat? Over at Chino's?"

"What he do this time?"

"Mouthed off to one of the bartenders. He was hanging around with Duane, Lisa's kid, you know, the—" and Uncle Ronnie flicked his wrist down in an exaggerated gesture and puckered his lips. "And when they saw that, they shot their mouths off at him and he shot his mouth back and it all ended with him limpin his ass out the bar, that fag probably kissin his wounds and suckin his dick all the way home."

They all laughed at that.

"He don't have a dad, though. That's what happens. God knows I love my sister, but—she can't handle that fucker. Not all on her own."

"And that goddamned hair!"

"I hate to say it, but maybe jail'd do him some good."

"Jail? Ship his ass overseas! Army'd knock him straight."

I stopped listening because just then Jay appeared outside the party, just beyond the circle of flame, like some kind of omen or vision. I was the only one who saw him. Everyone else was too engaged with their talk or the dumbass can game. He wasn't alone. A hooded shadow followed him into the shed where the bike rested like a dozing hellhound. The hair at the nape of my neck stood up and a breeze sent the autumn cold through my hoodie. I wiped my nose, set down my can of warm beer, and headed to the shed. Nobody seemed to notice.

I didn't know how drunk and fucked up I was until I stood up. Everything was sharp and dull, tall and small at the same time. It felt like the fire was hot on my heels. The dying leaves hissed long after the wind blew through them. My cousins' stupid laughter clanged and echoed in my head like bells far off in the distance. I stumbled my way up the path.

The shed twisted up like an abandoned church. I pushed open the door just wide enough to see inside. It was dark, but some firelight from the pit made its way through the dirty panes of the

window and I could see Jay bent over the seat of his bike. The figure behind him had his pants halfway down his thighs, so his bare
ass was showing and he was rutting into Jay with all the chaos of
an animal, his back twisted over like a question mark from having
to stand on his tiptoes to get at Jay. You could hear both of them
trying to stay quiet, except for one moment when Jay let out something halfway between a sigh and a whimper. That noise tacked
itself onto me like a wraith and I quietly shut the door and rejoined
the circle of men around the fire.

A few minutes later, the shed exploded to life with the crack
of the bike's pipes, and everyone about shit their pants. The doors
flew open and Jay ripped out of the driveway, that stranger with the
hood clinging hard to his back.

"Goddamn," my uncle Ronnie said over his cigarette. And then
all the men turned back to the fire.

THE NEXT MORNING, Jay was gone. His clothes and stash of cash,
all of it missing. I went back to the shed, stupidly thinking he'd
moved all his shit in there, but his bike was gone, too.

It broke my grandma more than she'd ever let on. More and
more nights, she wouldn't go to bed and started falling asleep on
her chair. I'd come home to find a cigarette dangling from her hand
over the rugs or the polyester arms of the recliner, threatening to
engulf the house in flames. Sometimes, when she did manage to get
to her bedroom, she'd call in sick the next day and sleep in her heap
of sheets way past noon. I started digging in her purse and going to
the grocery store alone.

I tried to change her memories about Jay, using the same trick I
used to change my own memories, but it was a dark trick, because

she started slipping and calling me his name, even when she was sober. Mostly she cried silently on the porch. I'd watch her from the screen door, the tears rolling down her cheek one at a time, like rationed coins for lost souls.

For a couple years after, before I moved out of my grams's and actually started trying for things like my GED and community college, I'd sometimes think about the last time I saw Jay, and I wondered if it was real. Whenever I was fucked up and some guy was suckin me off or I was busy with some girl I'd just met, sometimes I'd catch myself making the noise I heard him make, and when I did, I would know exactly where he was. Or I'd know exactly where he'd been. And sometimes I'd even know where he was going next.

———————

Damitri Martinez (he/his) is a 2019 Lambda Fellow. His work has appeared in *Foglifter* journal, where he is also an assistant editor. He is currently working on a collection of short stories and a novel. He lives in Denver, Colorado. To learn more, visit damitrimartinez.com.

EDITOR'S NOTE

For many years *Granta* has partnered with Commonwealth Writers to publish the five regional winners of their Commonwealth Short Story Prize—one each from Africa, Asia, the Caribbean, the Pacific, and Canada and Europe. It's a prize that gives a platform to places isolated from the traditional infrastructure of publishing, and through it we've had the chance to publish a range of brilliant new voices—among these is Mbozi Haimbe.

Her "Madam's Sister" is a brilliantly voiced story about class and community, which won the Commonwealth Short Story Prize for Africa in 2019. With a light touch, an ear for dialogue, and an intuition for the pattern of thought, Haimbe brings us into the world of Cephas, the gardener and security guard at a wealthy home, where he is employed by a woman referred to only as "Madam."

Cephas's world is one where the smell of honeysuckle mixes with that of the open-air sewer, where the naked lightbulbs at home contrast the four-by-four parked behind the heavy gate he mans at work. Small acts of generosity sustain the precarious community he is part of: to the neighbors who can't afford their electricity, even on payday; or to the grandmother who breaks rocks by the side of the road, hoping to sell enough to the construction sites to keep hold of what little furniture she possesses.

It takes real talent to conjure up the moral complexities these characters face every day with such naturalness, and to leave your reader experiencing the same sense of fatalism that they do.

Luke Neima, Digital Director and Online Editor
Granta

MADAM'S SISTER

Mbozi Haimbe

ELINA, THE MAID, is doing her thing of standing in a nice shaded spot on the veranda, while I stew in the heat. I carry on sweeping the paved front yard, sweat trickling down my back. The flagstones are patterned with black oil stains from the cars that park here at day's end. I pass my straw broom over these patches that refuse to be cleaned, even with water and soap. They make me look bad, lazy.

"Hey, Cephas . . . Cephas. Hey, Mr. Nyambe, it's you I'm talking to. Did you hear what I said? Madam's sister, the one who lives in the U.K., she's coming at the end of the week. You better move your lazy bones and clean this yard, yah? Make sure it shines London-style."

My hand tightens on the broom. One: I'm not lazy. How can I be lazy, me? I'm the gardener. I'm the guard. I'm the car washer. And also the odd-job man for all four households within the gated cluster of detached houses.

Two: Shine London-style. I can't even begin to interpret Elina's demand. How can an oily forecourt bordered by a threadbare lawn and dusty shrubs shine like London?

"Did you hear me, Cephas? I said . . ."

"Yes, yes. Okay. London-style," I say, swapping the broom for the hosepipe.

I aim a jet of water at the shrubs to wash the dust off their heat-curled leaves. Elina goes back inside, leaving me to wonder why Madam's sister is arriving at such short notice, making extra work for some of us. I also wonder what she looks like, for I have never seen her before. Is she dark, plump, and pleasant like Madam? I hope so, to the last part, at least.

The sun hammers down on me as midday approaches. I shift to stand under a tree and frown at the purple jacaranda blossoms peppering the lawn around the tree. Another task for me. But not for today. I lean my shoulder against the tree trunk, skin chafed by the rough bark. Still, I lean against that tree, and close my eyes. Maybe I doze a little, sleeping on my feet as the hosepipe hangs loosely from my fist.

"Cephas! Cephas, come and help me in here."

What does Elina want now? She's worse than all the other maids put together. Always wants help with this and that but never shares her wages. I pretend not to hear her, keep my eyes closed.

THE NEXT TWO days are brutal. I help Elina in the house: washing the curtains, washing the walls, and dabbing paint over the worst bits. I often help with odd jobs in Madam's house. Never has it smelt so clean, of soap and fresh air; never have the floors and windows sparkled quite like this. Madam drops in at lunchtime with bags and bags of shopping. She darts out again without a greeting or a smile, which is unlike her. Sweat studs her brow, wet patches spreading in semicircles where her dark blouse hugs her underarms.

I trot after her, in case there's more shopping to bring or in case she'd like me to close the gate after her. It's bad enough I wasn't at my post, forcing her to open the gate herself. There's only one more bag, which she hands off to me before hopping into her four-by-four. It's huge, black, and she revs the engine in unspoken impatience.

"Thank you for helping Elina," she takes time to say, before tearing out of the yard.

I blame Madam's sister for all this upset; all this rush-rush. This VIP treatment. Very Important Pest, if you ask me.

"Have you met the sister before?" I ask Elina back inside, helping her put away the shopping.

"Yes, ten years ago before she went to London. But not since then. She didn't even come home for their mother's funeral. Madam was most upset."

Well, like I said. Very important pest.

We stuff the fridge and freezer with luxury foods previously only admired on the shelves of Shoprite. Madam is usually an nshima, a meat-and-cabbage type. Here we have cheeses, apples, pears and other exotic fruits, cake, deli meats, all sorts. Saliva floods my mouth. I haven't had lunch yet. It's Elina's week to provide my lunch, but I see nothing happening on the stove.

"Cephas, can you help me to—"

"No," I say, heading for the back door. "All this helping you, and who's going to help me?"

Nobody helps finish the chores waiting for me outside. Not even the night security man who arrives at six. He parks himself in the guard hut, radio blaring its tinny disturbance. It's after seven by the time I'm done; too dark to see if the place is shining London-style.

The notes in my pocket are not for wasting on transport. I walk the five miles home, trying to ignore the pebbles slipping into my shoe through a hole in my sole. I'll have to get a new secondhand pair after payday.

I'm getting close to home. I'd know it even if the streetlights weren't showing me the way. It's in the thick smell as I leave behind the yards where I work, and approach Mumana, the komboni I've lived in since my grandmother took me in. The smell of green water wending through the komboni, carving out islands where houses sit. Infested waterways carrying colorful rubbish around the islands to dump it in the open-air sewage treatment plant on the outskirts of Mumana.

The army cleaned Mumana up during the cholera outbreak last rainy season. A few weeks after the soldiers and cholera left, the green water and rubbish returned. So, yes, the air pollution and the music tell me I'm home. Storefronts lit up with naked lightbulbs. Dusty convenience shops and hair salons and barbershops, with Zhi General Dealers being the biggest and most prominent. But the ones doing the most trade are the taverns selling both legal and illegal alcohol, and playing frenetic music from the hottest artists. It makes me want to dance, the music, despite my sore foot in its pebble-filled shoe.

I veer away from the taverns. Not enough money for a drink. Not if I want to eat today. I stop at the head of a side street to buy a tomato, an onion, a bunch of greens, and a small bag of mealie-meal.

"I'm still waiting for my money for that chicken, Bo Nyambe," says the vendor.

"You'll have it on payday. Surely you can wait three more days, Auntie."

"I'll be waiting," she says, handing me the shopping. She's included an extra tomato for free.

"Thank you. Payday, I promise."

My house is a little farther along the side street. It's a room attached to a row of six other rooms with shared bathroom and toilet facilities round the back, and a section of green stream behind the bathroom block. Chipo has the brazier going on the veranda of our room, a pot of water boiling on the blazing charcoal. She's talking to the neighbor across the narrow street but stops when she sees me and comes over to take the little bag of shopping.

"What time is this, Cephas? You're so late."

"Madam's sister—"

"Should pay you a bonus when she arrives."

I've been thinking about this very thing over the past two days, all the overtime I've worked. "I'm sure Madam will put something extra in my pay packet."

Chipo's too busy making dinner to reply. We eat out on the veranda like all of our neighbors and douse the charcoal ready to dry in the sun tomorrow for reuse. Only one of the neighbors has a bulb on, having topped up his electric meter. The rest of us call out to each other, chatting in the semi-gloom until the mosquitoes finally drive us inside.

Chipo lights a candle. The dancing flame shows her tired eyes and drawn face. I'm wise enough not to mention this. Chipo takes a lot of pride in her appearance, especially selling bananas and peanuts at the traffic lights on the big road not far from here. Greater chance of motorists buying from her if she looks presentable, she believes.

"You changed your hair. It looks nice," I say.

She smiles, running a hand over her hair, which is down to her shoulders. "This recycled weave? If only it could be Brazilian."

I've heard all about this Brazilian human hair during salon

sessions Chipo and her friends have on our veranda every now and then. They sit weaving wedges of hair into their cornrows with needle and thread while talking about how so-and-so from behind the market has a hundred-percent Brazilian swaying down her back, and how she must have found herself some sugar daddy or how else could she have afforded it? Thousands of kwacha, it costs. Chipo and I would both have to save our wages for three months and not pay rent in order to get Chipo some Brazilian. I'm suddenly exhausted. Or maybe I'm sick of never being able to give my beautiful wife the things she deserves. I lean over and blow out the candle, and, taking her hand, navigate around the couch to the back of the room.

"Let's go to bed," I say.

The mosquitoes whine in the darkness, the bedsprings creak, and my fingers snag in the waxy, synthetic strands of Chipo's weave.

I DROP THE rake and spring forward to answer the urgent honking at the gate. Madam's huge four-by-four rumbles through, hardly waiting for me to get the gate all the way open. I swallow down the swear word burning in my throat, forcing my face into an expression of neutral acceptance. The whole thing makes sense a second later when Madam climbs out of the passenger side. She wasn't the one driving; she'd never be that rude.

"Afternoon, Cephas."

I stand at attention. "Good afternoon, Madam."

From the driver's side emerges the sister, I presume. She looks like Madam, but is several shades lighter and several centimeters taller. Madam could not squeeze into her sister's tight jeans and tighter blouse or walk in her high-heeled boots. The sister has a

headful of fine hair down to the small of her back. The golden
color of maize silk, her weave is not stiff and waxy like Chipo's, but
moves in the breeze. This must be the famous Brazilian. The sister
tosses her head, sending all that silk swinging in the air. She's a vision, to be sure. With red, pouty lips and thick, long eyelashes and
blue eyes. Yes, blue. She's shining, London-style. The oil-stained
yard is not worthy of her.

"Hello? Get my bags, please," she says to me.

Mute, I tug open the boot and lift out the first suitcase. She has
six big bags in total. Just how long is she staying?

Madam and her sister go inside while I follow behind with two
of the bags. Elina shows me where to put the bags in the spare
room. The windows are wide open, letting in the sweet smell of
honeysuckle from the trellis in the back garden. The vines are a little overgrown. I've been meaning to trim them back, but the VIP's
arrival got in the way.

"Cephas! What about the rest of these bags," calls Elina.

"Coming," I mutter.

In the living room, the sister is stretched out on the couch, fan-
ning her face with a hand. Her nails are painted the same bright red
as her lips. She frowns, and groans about the heat and says she had
forgotten how hot Lusaka gets in October. It does get hot. A sort
of sticky, concentrated heat that makes the asphalt go soft. I ferry
the rest of the bags while Madam's sister fans her face, watching me
from the corner of her eye with that cool blue gaze.

I GET MY pay packet; there's no bonus in it. I daren't tell Chipo.
Instead, I pay the vendor for the chicken I got on credit, then get
another one on credit and allow Chipo to believe I bought it with

my bonus. She laughs and jokes with the neighbors as she fries the chicken. Almost all the other neighbors are cooking something tasty in their pots, judging from the cooking smells: chicken or beef or pork.

Our opposite neighbor isn't cooking at all. Ambuya's inside the house, door closed, with her two little grandchildren whose Chinese father went back to China after the smallest one was born. Then, soon after the father left, Ambuya's daughter said she was going to buy milk for the baby, and I don't know if she bought the milk or not, but she never came back.

My brother and I were once like those two boys, although our parents didn't just disappear. They died one after the other, and our grandmother was the only one left to look after us. She did her best, raising us in the room I still rent. There were days when the brazier was empty of coal and the door closed to block out the tantalizing smell of other people's payday cooking, and a hunger so deep and gnawing, it made you cry in your sleep. Despite all that, my grandmother still managed to put my brother and me through school.

"Cook extra nshima," I now tell Chipo.

She trades the small pot for a bigger one, lips tightening. "Cephas," she admonishes, "we can't feed the whole of Mumana."

All the same, when the food is cooked, a good portion of the chicken set aside for tomorrow, Chipo calls out to our opposite neighbor.

"Ambuya! Ambuya! Come, let's eat. I've cooked for you. Please come."

The door creaks open. "Thank you, my child, but I've already eaten. Maybe these two little ones, if you don't mind."

Her grandchildren run out of the house and cross the street, washing their hands in the bowl of water Chipo holds out. Usual murmur of conversation as we eat, neighborly banter from all sides. Except this time, only Ambuya's house is in darkness, all the other rooms on the crowded row lit by naked lightbulbs. Payday electricity.

MADAM'S SISTER STANDS around on the veranda, smoking or talking into her phone, or sometimes both. She charges around in Madam's car, driving in and out of the gates at least five times a day. After a week of this, Madam climbs into the driver's seat with determination stamped on her face.

"I need this car for work," she tells her sister, who is glaring at her with narrowed eyes from the edge of the veranda. "Take a taxi."

"From where? There are no taxis round here."

"Out of the gate, turn left, walk to the bottom of the road. Plenty of taxis there."

"Wait two seconds, let me just get ready and you can drop me at the taxi place."

"Wait? No, sorry. I'm already late for work," says Madam. "Bye!"

Madam's sister watches the car go, before turning her glare on me. I close the gate and go around to the back garden, away from the glare. A few hours later, at almost midday, insistent rapping sounds at the gate. Stone against metal, a relentless *rap-rap-rap*. No one behaves this way in Madam's neighborhood. Certainly, the hawkers know to knock once, then wait. I make my way to the front yard but bite back the rebuke I'd been about to unleash. There's Madam's sister, bashing a stone against the gate, leaving little pockmarks on the surface.

"Open this gate, please, guard," she says.

It would have been a simple matter for her to open it herself.

"Sorry, Madam," I say, getting it for her. It's my job, after all.

She totters down the road in her boots with the pointy heels, stumbling on the rocks all along the side of the road before taking to the tarmac like every other pedestrian. Except, who wears high, pointy-heeled boots to walk on the melting, hell-hot asphalt? Who does that? Not the other pedestrians, for sure. She gets stuck several times, and has to hop to get unstuck, great mane of blond Brazilian weave flopping about with her exertions. I'm not the only spectator, and not the only one laughing. I duck behind the gate when she turns around. Soon she's knocking to be let back in.

"Can you go get me a taxi?" she asks me.

Well, will she pay me a tip? Not likely. "Sorry, Madam. I'm not allowed to leave my post, in case of emergency."

She narrows her eyes as if to ask: "What kind of emergency?" But she doesn't challenge me, and I feel a spike of glee at winning this very minor skirmish.

I don't see much of Madam's sister after this . . . I lie; I do see snatches of her when I go inside to do odd jobs for Elina. She, the sister, would be painting her nails, or stretched on the couch watching TV while smoking and drinking red wine.

ONE DAY I'M changing a bulb in the kitchen when Madam's sister comes in, yelling. She looks wild. Her face is flushed, her lipstick smeared and her clothes rumpled. She has one blue and one brown eye, and she's shaking a small plastic box at Elina.

"I told you not to touch my things! Didn't I tell you not to touch my things? Now you've broken my contact lens."

Elina backs up against a kitchen cabinet, shaking her head, eyes wide. "Broken your what?"

"My contact. Don't pretend you don't know. My contact lens. It's all ruined thanks to you!"

"It's not me. It wasn't me," says Elina.

"Then who?" asks the sister. She's puffed up with ire, looks ready to strike. "Who, if not you?"

There's honking at the gate. Elina helps me for once, running out after me to tow open one side of the gate. Her eyes are shiny with tears. She doesn't go back inside but leaves right after closing her half of the gate.

Madam, who'd driven in, stares after her with a puzzled frown. "What happened? Is Elina all right?"

"The madam inside lost something, I think."

Madam draws a deep breath. "I see. Thank you, Cephas."

She goes inside, slamming the door so hard the windows rattle. Next, the shouting starts. I hear only Madam's voice; it seems the sister used up her shouting batteries while attacking Elina. I draw closer to the veranda, the better to hear through the open windows. Madam rants about the smoking and drinking and spoiled-brat routine.

"When are you going to grow up? You're over thirty, an old woman. Time to act your age. And let me catch you harassing my staff again, you will see my bad side. You will see it," says Madam. The next second, two packs of cigarettes fly out the window. "Smoke out there before you kill us all, for goodness' sake!"

Iye. I never knew Madam had such a temper. I leave, before she catches me eavesdropping and shows me her bad side.

———

CHIPO DOESN'T HAVE the brazier going when I arrive home today. Her supply of bananas and roasted peanuts is spoiling, she says. We eat the blackened bananas and stale peanuts, slapping at the mosquitoes that needle our arms and legs. Across the road, one of the children is crying and calling to his grandmother.

"Ambuya, Ambuya. Wake up!"

I glance at Chipo, the food somehow now tasting too spoiled to swallow. Ambuya has seemed a little older of late, a lot more tired. She breaks rocks with a hammer by the side of the road, selling the resulting stones to those people building houses. It's not easy work for an elderly lady.

"Someone should check on her," says Chipo.

I don't want to be the one to do it. One of our older neighbors, silently volunteering, goes into Ambuya's darkened house. The crying stops. Soon, the grandchildren scamper out, coming straight to Chipo. She croons and rocks them, and takes them into our room when the neighbor comes out of Ambuya's house, asking someone to fetch the police.

OUR ROW OF houses collects some money. It's not much, but it will hold things together until Ambuya's son arrives from the Copperbelt tomorrow. Us neighbors and Ambuya's friends from church gather at her house: the men on the veranda, the women inside. The grandchildren cling to Chipo, and the green smell clings to all of us. It's getting worse. It always gets worse just before an outbreak of something deadly. Some of the mourners are whispering that the cholera's back.

"That's how it starts," they say, "with the old women and the babies."

At times like this, I'd like a big car like Madam's so that I could drive away and leave the network of green streams behind forever. Leave the crowded streets and noisy taverns and corner street vendors and their credit chickens. Leave, like my brother Patrick did. He lives in a yard bigger than Madam's. A yard with only one house, not a cluster of houses. His guard works only for him, not for three other households.

I huddle closer to the brazier and hold out my hands to the warmth, even though I'm not particularly cold. I got better grades than Patrick; I could've gone to university, too. But I wanted money now-now. So I found work as a security guard. Patrick went to university and was broke for four years. He's not broke now. Patrick doesn't get chicken on credit and can afford to buy his wife ten Brazilians.

"CEPHAS, WHERE HAVE you been for the past two days?"

"Sorry, Madam. I had a funeral. My grandmother died." It's kind of true. Ambuya was everyone's grandmother.

"Oh." Madam's frown dissolves. "My condolences. But please next time phone or send word."

"Yes, Madam."

She takes a few notes out of her purse, gives them to me, and for a moment her hand hovers like she's going to pat my shoulder in some cringe-making gesture of sympathy. Thankfully she reconsiders, and I escape to open the gate. Elina's been watching the awkward exchange from the veranda. She makes a clicking sound in her throat, mild disapproval, and goes back to applying polish on the veranda floor.

"What's your problem, you?" I ask, keeping a few steps away

from the veranda. The polish smells like industrial-grade paraffin, makes me queasy.

"Your grandmother died a long time ago, iwe, Cephas. Lying is a sin, ka. Sinner man."

"Yes, keep talking. Keep annoying me. I'll call the sister to come and shut you up."

Elina laughs, completely recovered from the drama, it seems. "Ya, ya, ya. She's mad, that one. Ati contact lens. A blue one, for that matter. Do I look like someone who's got time for blue eyes?"

I'd like to stand around laughing with Elina, but the work has mounted during my two days away. Leaves to rake, lawn to water, trellis to trim. It's afternoon before I get around to tackling the trellis in the back garden. The heat is like a blanket wrapped around me, humid, suffocating. I'd like a glass of ice water. I'd like a cold shower. What I get is the sting of sweat in my eyes and sunburn on the back of my neck. I hack at the honeysuckle, vicious like I'm stabbing a witch. Quite by accident, my gaze wanders to the window of the room where I brought the sister's bags weeks ago.

I stop hacking.

She's asleep, her face turned away from the open window. On the pillow beside her is the Brazilian. A wig. Not a weave. The sister's own hair is done up in intricate cornrows as thin as a needle, nice enough. But the prize, the bonus, is that length of silk three times my wages and Chipo's combined. Madam's sister is from London: she's rich. She can easily buy another wig. A man like me, on the other hand, I'll never get another chance to give my beautiful Chipo this one thing she desires; a thing she deserves.

I reach through the window.

Madam's sister keeps sleeping.

I grab the thing and go back to work with it tucked under my shirt. It's insanely hot work, hacking at a honeysuckle bush with a full head of hair nestled against your chest.

ONCE AGAIN, CHIPO doesn't have food going when I get home but instead sits on a little wooden stool next to the lifeless brazier. There's mealie-meal and kapenta in the house, cooking oil, onions, tomatoes. Why hasn't she cooked?

"Why haven't you cooked?" I ask, my plan to whip out her present from under my shirt on hold.

Chipo stares at the house across the street. It's lively again with the noise of a new family moving in. On the veranda, a woman threatens to smack a girl who's dancing around a blazing brazier with a sizzling pan on it.

"The Copperbelt uncle took Ambuya's bed and table," says Chipo. "He left the boys. They cried and cried."

This sometimes happens. Property grabbed, children abandoned. I lean back against the wall, scratching an itchy spot on my belly under the wig.

"Where are they now?"

"Ambuya's church friend took them to the school," says Chipo.

An orphanage in the community. "They'll be all right there. We can go see them sometime."

Not looking at all convinced, she stands up and turns her back on the happy family across the street. "I'll prepare you some food." Chipo's voice is dull, her shoulders slumped.

I touch her cheek to stop her from going inside, and say, "It's okay, we'll eat at the tavern. Madam gave me some money."

Interest sparks in her eyes. "Really?"

"Yes, really." I pull the wig from its hiding place. "She also gave me this. Why don't you go and bathe, then put it on?"

Chipo clutches the wig, strokes it, laughs, high-pitched. "Brazilian? Oh, Cephas! Thank you, thank you."

At the tavern, Chipo tosses her head and runs her fingers through her hair, and makes sure her friends get a feel of it to verify it's the real thing. I'm content to watch her being so happy. We eat nshima and T-bone steak, and drink all the money Madam gave me, and dance to the latest tunes, Chipo preening like the most beautiful peacock that ever lived.

LATE TO WORK, bleary-eyed, head pounding. Madam's also late for work, I notice. Her car's still parked in its usual place. I doze while watering the grass under the jacaranda tree. The tiny flowers on the lawn are brown, sad and withered, purple no more. Elina leaves the veranda to come and talk to me. I can guess what she's going to say.

"Madam's sister has lost her wig. Imagine."

I try to act surprised. It's not easy. "Lost her wig? But how?"

"Who knows? She's always drunk; she could've left it any-where." Elina darts a glance at the living room windows, lowers her voice. "She hasn't stopped crying about it. Real tears."

"Is that why Madam hasn't gone to work, because of the cry-ing?" I ask.

"Over a silly wig. Some people."

We both shut our mouths when Madam's sister storms out onto the veranda. Barefoot, her clothing wine-stained. She lights a ciga-rette and paces; she puffs and paces. Yelling at Madam through the window in between puffs. She has recharged her shouting batteries, definitely.

"Don't you get it? How thick are you? I can't go back. I have no papers. What you see on me, and in those suitcases, it's all I have. It's everything. It's ten years of my life. Just a wig?" She laughs, hysteria in her voice. "You have no idea how tough it really is."

"What's she talking about?" whispers Elina.

I shrug. "I don't know. Some newspapers?"

I do know that Madam's sister can't shout forever. Still, I block out her yelling, and water the plants, rake the lawn. Count down the hours till I can go home and rest my pounding head.

Mbozi Haimbe was born and raised in Lusaka, Zambia. She writes African-inspired realist and speculative fiction. Mbozi completed a Master of Studies in Creative Writing at the University of Cambridge in 2018 and is currently working on her debut novel. "Madam's Sister" was a regional winner of the Commonwealth Short Story Prize in 2019. Mbozi is a social worker and lives in Norfolk, England, with her family.

EDITOR'S NOTE

"Don't Go to Strangers" is rare for its depth and humanity, and demonstrates formidable powers of both observation and, just as essential, empathy. Matthew Jeffrey Vegari traces the intricate nuances of not one but two marriages, and the slippery tensions, sorrows, and unexpected passions among those four characters. The point of view moves gracefully from one character to the next, while the scope is contained to one late, intoxicated evening. Through that focused lens, the reader gets a panoramic overview that is nevertheless intimate in its observation. The exquisitely developed interiority of all four characters, whose competing (if unspoken) needs bring them inevitably, though subtly, into conflict, generates the narrative's quiet tension. There is, for each protagonist, the ache of a loss, a worry, a vulnerability, or an unmet desire they carry through their days. It's the precision and tenderness with which Vegari renders those aches that makes this piece memorable.

It was an easy editorial decision to accept this story, and we were proud to see Matthew Jeffrey Vegari join the illustrious roster of writers whose first professional publication was in ZYZZYVA.

Laura Cogan, Editor
ZYZZYVA

DON'T GO TO STRANGERS

Matthew Jeffrey Vegari

IN THE LIVING room, two couples sit on opposite leather couches, one hand-in-hand, fingers laced around fingers, the other slightly apart, shoe heels touching on the shag carpet below. Another dinner party of friends and coworkers has ended, and the couples carry on even as they begin to forget their words. The women finish off tall glasses of champagne; the men gulp down warm bottles of beer. It is after ten. Everyone has gone home for the evening, with the exception of Alice and Trevor Jackson, who do not overstay their welcome. On the contrary, the hosts, Allen and Jane Mitchell, are pleased to have friends linger behind. Between the marriages of the Jacksons and Mitchells there are three girls and a boy, two children per couple, who are upstairs sleeping in the case of the Mitchells, or, for the Jacksons, a few miles east, watching a movie with a babysitter who has been told that things could end at any hour.

Allen Mitchell takes a final sip of his beer and squeezes his wife's hand. It has been a long day for them both, and now they can relax and enjoy a drink or two, maybe a slice of cake. They worked hard to entertain twenty people in their home, and things went well—very well, in fact. The guests arrived on time; dinner was served without complaint; the thunderstorm, once predicted to ruin the evening, postponed itself for another day. Allen looks across the room to Trevor, who is telling a story about two of his students, one he has told before, about a spontaneous wrestling match. Allen appreciates that his friend of many years can enjoy this night with him. He has known Trevor through their graduations, high school and college, and their weddings, and tonight the celebration of his own promotion registers another victory. In a way, he thinks, they are like brothers. He has seen Trevor grow from a young boy with a thin frame to a towering man, a father, with large arms and a sizeable stomach. And, much like brothers, their relationship has changed over time, too. Last week, after discussing Trevor's upcoming thirty-sixth birthday over lunch, he became conscious of a pause in their conversation—a lull—as the two of them looked out the window and chewed their sandwiches. He found comfort in the familiarity of their friendship, a friendship that eliminated the need to say anything at all. The silence itself was full.

Jane laughs at Trevor's story, one that gets funnier each time he tells it. She looks from Trevor to Alice, who grins uncomfortably, perhaps worried that her husband's old joke will fall flat. Jane is not fond of Alice Jackson but appreciates how her own husband gets along with Trevor. Trevor is taller than Allen, better at sports, the one prone to overdrinking at gatherings like this. Allen is smarter and handsomer, his hair showing no signs of thinning. Trevor is a gym teacher and Allen is, now, a vice president. Unlike the two men, however, Jane and Alice do not complement each other. Their friendship was not formed organically, and instead they met out of an expectation for spouses. As she knows many people do, Jane maintains her friendship with Alice out of convenience: for the sake of their husbands, it is simply easier to be friends than adversaries. Not for the first time this evening, she wonders what a man like Trevor sees in a woman like Alice, a woman whose nose bends at the tip and whose cheeks engulf her small eyes. She is a good mother, Jane thinks, but a hostile woman.

Allen removes his hand from Jane's manicured fingers and secures two more beers from the outdoor cooler. Under the white container lid, the bottles float in tepid water, their labels peeling off like dead skin. He searches for lime wedges and grows frustrated in the dim light. He turns and knocks on the window, but Jane calls out and shakes her head, pointing across the house. The limes are in the kitchen—he is too lazy to retrieve them. Trevor won't mind. Allen closes the door to the patio and re-enters the house, watching a few moths flutter to the light fixture above. Even when they leave the screen door closed, the moths find their way inside. His wife is right: if the bugs will intrude regardless, better to remove the wire mesh entirely. It is ugly.

Alice tacitly agrees to stay late so that her husband can have a good time. He works hard, and, unlike her, has only one close friend in Allen. Trevor is introverted until he drinks, so she takes it upon herself to find new restaurants and outings when things get slow. There are a few reservations and parties lined up in the coming weeks, but the Mitchells are their closest friends. Alice doesn't like Jane, but company is company. Like her, Jane is an only child, and both their fathers have died. There is some comfort in their histories, though not much else. Alice is unyielding, hardworking, disciplined. Jane is carefree, less organized, and equally happy. For their husbands, they sometimes meet for walks and always exchange gifts on birthdays.

"Wouldn't you rather go on a nice vacation once or twice a

year," Jane asks, twirling the stem of her champagne glass, "than buy a cabin—a *cabin!*—that doesn't let you go anywhere else and forces you to spend money on repairs and upkeep?"

Alice looks at her watch, a Timex purchased on sale. She realizes that Allen must have gotten a fairly big raise at work. She wonders what it means to go from regional manager to vice president. She dislikes the Mitchells for this arrogance; it was typical of them to make it hard to say congratulations. Allen may have been promoted, but nothing fundamental has changed. Tonight is business as usual for the Mitchells as they brag of their own successes and prevent the nice evening from speaking for itself.

"Wouldn't you rather go," Jane continues, "to Paris, London, Tokyo?"

Alice wants to reply with the frankness that a question like that deserves: of course she'd rather travel! Of course she'd rather have a cabin in the woods! For her and her husband, it isn't a matter of preference. It is a matter of having the opportunity for preference. But, to at once challenge Jane and keep up their façade, she tells her that she'd rather have a cabin. Because if the Mitchells invited them for a weekend, they would be able to go. She thinks to add that they should make sure to have a guest bedroom, but that's a little on the nose. Besides, she doesn't actually want to go on vacation with the Mitchells.

Allen decides not to hold Jane's hand when he sits back down. She brought up the new house even though he told her to wait for another night. He genuinely wants to know the Jacksons' opinion, but this is too much. They held a dinner party to celebrate, and his wife just gave away the extent of his new salary. It's a significant raise but not an unexpected one. His boss told him to be proud of the promotion, of the achievement. To mark the occasion more permanently, he already bought a new grill, a Weber, the expensive kind with six burners. He understands that a second house is so much more than a grill, almost like having another child. He can see Alice growing uncomfortable. He spies the straightening of her spine, the smoothing of her dress across her lap.

Jane doesn't know why she brought up the new house. She often compares drinking to getting in the pool: she's cold for a moment and then warm all over. She admits that she shouldn't have said anything, and that Allen specifically warned her of this, but Alice was sitting there, smugly, making her silent criticisms. Soon, Jane knows, Alice will make a comment that provokes them all. So there is something satisfying about a preemptive strike, about flipping the script, even if it is too easy, even if tomorrow she will regret embarrassing herself. She can never point to the exact moment in the night when Alice spoils the fun, but like the light outside, there is a slow change in color, from a warm yellow to a cold black, until the only sources of light are the individual flashes from fireflies: Trevor, Allen, and her. And though she doesn't know how it got to be so dark, she knows who is responsible.

Trevor is surprised by his happiness for Allen. On some level, he feels that he, too, has been given a promotion, though on what merit he can't say. Maybe for being a good friend. Maybe for pretending that he doesn't know his wife hates the Mitchells. Alice says she hates Jane only because of her coyness, but he knows the truth: his wife hates the successes of others. *Hate*, he realizes, is too strong a word, but he likes to deal in extremes. It is why he always drinks too much, works too hard, angers too easily; why he was the best linebacker in high school and college, while simultaneously at risk for losing his scholarship; why he has only one very good friend.

"We were discussing, you know, the *issue* again last week," Alice says, placing her hand on her husband's leg and noticing the tiniest stain just below his knee.

"Babe, not now," Trevor says. "And it's not an 'issue.'"

"No, no. I want to know what they think. What do you think *now* about us having another baby?"

"Well," says Jane.

"Oh," says Allen.

Jane wants to know why she has had this conversation three times in two years. Twice on Alice's birthday and once on a dinner date. There is no more she can say, but so much more she feels she must: Alice and Trevor do not have enough money; their marriage seems just stable enough to maintain the status quo; their two kids will be out of the house in fewer than ten years. Why would they start over now? Deep down, she knows that this has nothing to do with children. For Alice, children, and any other topic pulled from an imaginary catalogue she might call "Family," are but an excuse to have a conversation with others, a dialogue so that she feels present and acknowledged. Jane's mother, a psychiatrist, told her so during a visit a few months ago. Her mother has many theories about many people but this one is particularly insightful. Jane has mentioned this to Allen in passing only once, worried that her mother will come across worse than Alice. Tomorrow—and she hopes she will remember the precise way to say it—her husband will learn more of what she really thinks of Alice Jackson. She will say that Alice ruins these dinners with her questions, suffocating conversation with a thick blanket of too-personal topics, all under the guise of lighthearted intimacy. She will try to speak without hyperbole, to restrain herself as best she can, out of respect for Trevor. But Alice has embarrassed herself tonight, far more than her own comment, however calculated, about a new house. Alice talks as though her family inhabits a filing cabinet, color-coded by age and sex. These are not issues for the company of others. They are issues for—a therapist.

Allen makes an effort not to look amused, taking as many sips of his beer as he can manage. Trevor, he now remembers, warned him on a recent run that Alice might make a fool of herself: "When she asks, *if* she asks, say something about the kids being out of the house in a few years. Don't mention money. Never mention that." Allen promised that he would toe the party line. He thinks the Jacksons certainly *could* have another baby, but something has stayed with him since that conversation. He was sure he heard a tremor in his friend's voice, one that betrayed a great resistance to the notion of renewed parenthood. It was an almost biological response, and if Trevor had not already had two children, Allen would question his ability to conceive at all. Trevor had once been so adamant about having kids, about becoming a dad. Allen knows these ongoing troubles stem from a common source: the Jackson marriage, two people deeply at odds with each other. Through his wife, he has learned that Alice is happy as a mother, content with the ordinariness of her life and reluctantly accepting of the ordinariness of her partner. But Trevor, living under the same roof, seems caught in a long-lived jet lag, fatigued by something without remedy. "A kid can't solve problems," Trevor told him. "It only adds more."

Trevor feels himself loosening up, caring a little less about his wife's behavior. He knows it's the alcohol, and for a fleeting moment he wonders how he will be able to drive home. It is not so much a matter of falling asleep behind the wheel, or even feeling dizzy or lightheaded. He is simply not meant to drive this evening, to return home, but he will anyway, because he has made the trip before under worse circumstances and influences. He is almost finished with his beer and knows that the time has come for another. He steps outside onto the patio and lifts the lid of the cooler. They are drinking his favorite beer tonight, a grapefruit IPA, which means his friend bought it specifically for him. How nice, he thinks— who would not want to promote this man, who hosts these parties, spends so much money on his friends, and asks for little in return? Only his wife would object, out of envy.

"Maybe we can save this conversation for a different time," Allen proposes.

"You're right. Let's change the subject," Alice replies.

Alice doesn't want another baby. She frustrates herself and puts her marriage and friendships on edge for—she can't identify an immediate purpose. It just seems like the right way to fill the gap, like when she cuts the line at the store because the person in front of her is distracted and won't notice. She mentioned getting pregnant last week with her husband, just so that they could talk about *something*. She didn't see his face as he nodded uneasily, his fingers fumbling with the laces of his sneakers. She picked that moment deliberately so Trevor would have something to think and talk about on his run. She knows he tells Allen all the details of their relationship, the details the way he sees them, those things she would never confide in Jane. She brought up a topic, serious-seeming—a baby— because they have become a couple that remains silent at dinner, allowing their children to explain every thought in their heads, as though the things an eight- and ten-year-old have to say are somehow more meaningful and therefore worthier of conversation. She can't imagine what gets discussed in the Mitchell house, but they are the more cerebral couple. Allen and Jane both read the same books, watch the same shows, finish each other's thoughts. Alice isn't jealous, however. She tries to keep up, but Jane reads too much fiction. Alice sees her mouth in the reflection of her glass, her lips curling upward: the Mitchells read fiction because their lives need to be thrown into relief.

Jane tries to mention a new show that she and Allen are watching, a docuseries about a murder, but she remembers that Trevor does not watch television in the way that they do. He watches basketball and football, at the professional and college level, and sometimes pays attention to the news, because, she assumes, he feels that's what a person *should* do. She thinks he could have been a sports announcer, instead of a gym teacher. He has managed to stay fit, and despite filling out in the middle, he has never lost that look of a tight end. She wishes her own husband dressed like a commentator. Allen likes nice things (look at the grill he just bought), but his taste in clothes upsets her. Tonight Alice made a comment about his shirt not matching his jacket, a comment Jane could not disagree with, no matter its rudeness. Next week she will pick out what he wears to dinner when they all go out to celebrate Trevor's birthday. She should remember to arrange for the babysitter and to buy a gift, one that Allen will suggest. She is not looking forward to the dinner because the Jackson children will be there. They are nine and ten years old, the age when chatting with adults suddenly becomes appealing. She herself just had her second baby a few months ago, and her first two years before that, so she knows her children and the Jacksons' will not be friends. This is, of course, only true if Alice does not get pregnant again—though, who knows? By then, maybe they will have moved away or found new best friends.

Allen wonders how many beers are left the cooler; he worries that Trevor has had too much to drink. Not too much to drink given his height and weight, but too much to drink to drive home safely. Trevor can be reckless at parties, and if Allen tries to stop him from driving, there will be an argument and Trevor will win. Allen knows that his friend will yell, threaten to wake the neighbors in the houses next door, and that he himself will shake his head and close the front door, disappointed that it should always come to this. When Trevor drinks, he changes into a different person, no less likeable, possibly more likeable, but altogether different. More abrasive and intrusive. His size becomes apparent, because he becomes physical, harder to overlook. Alice, Allen has noticed, welcomes the difference, encourages it even, perhaps because the drunk Trevor becomes more the man she wishes he were: open and sociable, brutish and assertive. He would never tell that to Jane; he would never give her a reason to dislike Alice. He appreciates their friendship, admires it, because it makes these parties and dinners so much better. In truth, he has never understood how the two women get along. A few years ago he asked Trevor how they would manage with two wives so fundamentally different from each other. Trevor said that women could surprise you.

"Any new crazy students, Mr. Jackson?" Jane asks.

Trevor smiles. He looks at Jane with appreciation, as sincerely as possible, though the beers have relaxed the muscles in his face.

No one in the world appreciates his job as a teacher more than she does. At every meal, she asks about the students and the football team. It was Jane who saw when his name appeared in the local paper, who knew when the team had amassed a record number of points for their division, who attended the ceremony when he won an award for coaching. Allen, he admits, also supports him in this way, but for him there is a certain expectation. Jane, as far as he can tell, does not even like sports. She simply cares about him as a friend, as a good person, the kind of person Allen deserves.

Alice refills her glass, disappointed that the bubbles fail to spill over the rim. Does each sip of champagne toast Allen? She digs her feet into the shag carpet and stretches her legs forward. They have been at the Mitchells' house for almost five hours, and her husband has spoken about school too many times to count. She loves that he is a teacher, that he teaches students how to run, how to hit, how to throw a ball. But it's not as if Allen has nothing to talk about. Clearly he has stories of his own, stories of success worth celebrating with dinner parties. She does not want to hear about management at his financial firm or about Jane's work as a hospital administrator, but she knows that either topic is what they *should* be discussing. She is wearing nice shoes and drinking champagne. School is a topic that she hears about every day from her children. In time, the Mitchells will come to agree with her, when their own children ride the bus each morning. And, she thinks, they will wish they had spent these moments, moments of peace that come too infrequently, talking about something else.

"Did you hear about—I'm sure you know about it—but did you hear about that teacher at Ammons?" asks Allen.

"Oh, you know I hate that stuff," Jane replies.

"How old did they say the girl was?"

Jane watches Alice purse her lips. This has happened before, though she has never been too sure of the implications. Whenever a school scandal is brought up, Alice tries to redirect the conversation, as though she and Trevor are somehow involved. It must be a fear of Alice's, Jane thinks, that Trevor will have an affair with a female student and leave her alone to take care of their family. Jane's own fears are far different. She worries constantly about getting fired, about making an error that makes her look less competent than her peers. She waited weeks before announcing her second pregnancy despite the tightness of her clothes, her more measured gait. It was a silly thing to worry about because there were so many laws to protect her. But, to her disappointment, she has become far more self-conscious in the past year, particularly in the months since giving birth a second time. There has been a change in the way she moves, in the way she handles things, in the way she functions in their little world. She is now more grounded, more stable, but she wants to feel powerful again, carefree, like she can do anything at a moment's notice. She wants the added weight in her hips to fall away with a single stomp of her foot. "You just don't want responsibilities," her mother said. "You're describing youth, being young."

Alice tries hard not to think about these school scandals. Trevor would never do such a thing, would never think of doing such a thing, but still she worries. She worries more about what a young girl might say than what an older man might do. Her husband is exactly the kind of teacher that she would have found alluring as a high school student: tall, strong, married with children. Teenagers, she thinks, are not drawn immediately to people or physical features; they are drawn to ideas that lead to mistakes. She has overheard her husband and Allen discussing a teacher they once found attractive, a teacher with whom Trevor now works. The woman is no longer young enough to be the object of students' fantasies, though Alice has difficulty placing her in an attractive light at any age. It was merely the *idea* of sleeping with a teacher that had enticed Trevor and Allen twenty years ago. When she closes her eyes, she imagines a young girl, with breasts just large enough to be called breasts, looking at her husband and concocting a simple lie, the type of lie that can end a family, a marriage, your place in the community.

Allen holds Jane's hand once more, stroking the back of her thumb with his own. Her skin is always softer than his, no matter how much of her moisturizer he borrows. For many years, he assumed that this was a difference between men and women, that men have rough hands and women soft ones. But at work he has met women with hands rougher than his own. He laces his fingers with Jane's, tucking his thumb inside and stroking the inside of this makeshift pocket, her palm. How much longer will Trevor and Alice stay? He lets go of Jane's hand and moves his arm slowly, cautiously, to her back, careful not to distract her while she speaks. He makes figure eights against her dress with his forefinger, before dragging his hand up to her neck where he lightly pinches her nape. He hears a lilt in Jane's voice when he tickles her, though she gives no indication for him to stop. He hopes the Jacksons decide to leave.

"Listen to that thunder!" Trevor says. "The storm is coming after all. Better bring those beers inside."

"You just want an excuse for another drink," Alice replies.

"So what?"

"I'll grab you a lime," says Jane.

"I'll help you," says Allen.

Trevor pulls back the screen door and steps outside. He feels the wind picking up, shaking the vinyl cover of Allen's new grill. It's a large grill, sturdy, one that he would like to own himself. He picks up the cooler with both hands, more quickly than he should, and the water inside sloshes over the edge and onto his pants. That's all right, he thinks. Better than a bottle of wine! He walks back through the screen door and closes it behind him, cradling the container awkwardly in his arms. He realizes that he should drain the water out in the grass, so he opens the screen door once more, steps down the brick steps, and unplugs the white plastic spout. The water rushes out quickly. He tilts the container to let out the final drops. There are two beers left: one for him and one for Allen. They will try to get him to stop drinking, but it's September. He needs to enjoy these last days of summer. Let him have his fun.

Alice watches Trevor through the window, fumbling with the cooler like a little boy carrying something too big for his body. He has had too much to drink. Here is the proof: this wetness on his pants, so much wetness that in any other circumstance one would assume he poured water on himself intentionally, or even more embarrassing . . . How much longer will they stay? She checks her watch. It is close to midnight; they have been here longer than any other time, longer even than the time when Trevor passed out on the couch. She wonders if her husband drinks because that is what people do at parties like this, or because he needs to. The only test would be for Allen and Jane to have a dinner party every day. Then she could keep track of his behavior with a mental checklist, gauging his interactions with others, his liberal sips of beer.

"Do you think they'll leave sometime soon?" Allen asks in the kitchen.

"Shh, a minute. I'm listening to the monitor," says Jane.

"I told you we could have kept the babysitter longer."

"It was late, and she shouldn't have to stay just because of them."

"Well, what about *us*? What about, you know?"

Allen reaches over Jane's shoulder and pulls the monitor from her ear. He wraps his hand around her waist, pulling her body against his own. He feels the warmth between them, the arousal, the end of the night arriving on cue. How many years has he known her? She has had just enough to drink; he knows what comes next. Why has it become so hard to be parents and lovers? There are two babies upstairs, each a part of him, like limbs that ache and stir, parts that keep him from sleeping through the night. He often thinks of how simple they are, how animalistic: they eat, they sleep, they cry. He and Jane have joked about the way kids play in the park, shouting out half commands, falling over, hurting themselves. "They look drunk," Jane said last week. Allen holds the monitor close to his ear, waiting for the rise and fall of breath. There is always a moment of panic when he or Jane wants to run upstairs or into the next room, but if they wait long enough, the monitor will produce that sign of life, and they will know that all is well. Suddenly he hears music. He lets go of Jane, and they walk toward the living room. Trevor is swaying with Alice, who laughs and tries to keep his big shoes off her bare toes.

"I'm sorry, he said he wanted music!" says Alice.

Jane curls her arm around Allen's neck. She closes her eyes. This is what the night needed. A little night music! She smiles to herself. They are listening to an album she left in the stereo, an old CD she found at a yard sale. She hears the jazz, the buzz of the woman's voice, the thrum of fingers against the wooden bass. Caramel, she thinks. Rich, dark sugar swirling in the bottom of a pan. She can almost smell it.

"I love you," Allen whispers in her ear.

"Who is singing, Jane?" Alice asks.

"Her name is Etta Jones."

"Etta James, you mean."

"No, Etta James sings 'At Last.' This is Etta *Jones*. She's less known. Here, listen to this."

Jane pulls away from her husband and picks up the remote from the table. She bites her lip and changes the song. She can't remember the title or any of the lyrics. She never used to be this aware of alcohol, this conscious of a change in body temperature. She feels little bursts of heat rising under her skin, trapped pockets of warm air that she can't let out even as she presses against her face. She sees herself drinking, being drunk, as though there are two versions of her, the one changing the music with clicks of the remote and the one thinking of how difficult it is to make these tiny clicks. At what point should she stop drinking? Are there still rules for quantity, even after breastfeeding? No, there are no more rules besides those she sets for herself. She flips through the album, listening to each track for some thirty seconds. Alice sits down on the couch and sighs at the brief disruption in the music. It wouldn't be a proper party if she didn't give Alice something to complain about. But she will win this exchange, and the wait will have been worth it. Finally, she finds it. She hears the piano twinkling.

"This one. Listen to this one."

Trevor has not heard the song before but trusts Jane's taste in music. She has an ear for this sort of thing, more than Allen or his own wife. They have all gone to the theater before, and Jane is always the one who explains the backstory, why something is important, why they should be more appreciative than they are. She could have been a teacher, Trevor thinks. The song is beautiful; he can hear it now. What a voice this woman—not Etta James—had. He takes another sip of his beer, frowning at its flatness. Alice used to be a singer, he remembers. In college, he met many women who sang in the chorus or onstage, but Alice was different. She sang because she wanted to, not because she needed to be heard and wanted others to listen. She used to sing to their kids; she used to sing, softly, after they had sex and he would play with her hair.

"You're not gonna join me for this one?" Trevor asks.

"Maybe in a minute. I feel woozy," Alice answers.

"I won't leave you like that!" Allen jokes.

Jane sits down on the couch next to Alice, pleased that the song is as lovely as she remembers. She laughs when her husband puts his arm behind Trevor's back, so that they dance together like a couple. She looks at Alice and catches her smiling. They nod at each other in a silent exchange, a mutual understanding that this closeness between their husbands, formed through childhood, is why they are still up, though it's already past midnight. Trevor is the bigger man in the embrace, though it's unclear which of them, if either, is leading. Her husband leans against Trevor for support, a man propped against a wall. Trevor, despite having drunk the most, is now in control. His hand rests on the back of Allen's head. How funny, Jane thinks, that she has seen him toss her husband into the pool with ease. They are such different sizes, such different people. Her mother once told her to watch out for Trevor Jackson. She would never do such a thing—she isn't that kind of person.

Besides, what would an affair look like, sound like? "Half my patients have had affairs," her mother told her, "and none of them thought they ever would." A few years ago, it would have been unthinkable, but now Jane knows that moments do arise when a simple look or remark can mean so much more at thirty-five than it did at twenty-five. At twenty-five, everyone made those remarks, those flirtations, because that was what you did to show the world who you were becoming, who you would become. But now she has lost the ability to hide behind herself. She is a mother. Her first child tells her to sit, to come, to read a book. Alcohol brings back that bygone confidence for an hour until she remembers the truth. It is the exception that proves the rule. She wishes she could live her life two drinks in.

Alice hangs her head over her lap. She hopes that if she pretends to fall asleep, the night will end and she can return home to pay the babysitter, who has earned too much money for a single night. But no one notices her. She looks up at the dancing, if that is the right word. Her husband is whispering in Allen's ear, probably encouraging him to get to sleep. She knows that her eyes have widened, that her cheeks are stretched upward, that she feels something light inside, as though the night has decided to restart itself. It is the music, the alcohol, the end of a long day. She danced with Trevor for the first time in many months. But why does it feel like one dance can brighten the color of the walls, exaggerate the tickle of champagne bubbles against her upper lip? She loves this feeling, this lightness, more than anything else. Trevor will be thirty-six years old next week. They have been married for ten years, a decade. And, as everyone told her on her wedding day, the years really do start to go by faster. She tells herself not to be so sappy. She knows that wine and champagne have given, only to take away; this kind of happiness is false and short. She has compared it to when she nursed her children, to when they hug her, to when she sees them sing in the choir. Those feelings are the pure thing. Tonight she has danced and laughed under a spell, a cheap magic trick.

"'Make your mark for your friends to see. But when you need more than company, don't go to strangers. Come on to me.' God, I just love that," says Jane, squeezing Alice's hand.

"Yes, I heard it. Thank you for playing the song," Alice replies, smiling.

Allen smells Trevor's deodorant. It is crisp, wintry, like the middle of a forest. "Just another minute," he wants to say. The room spins and spins around him, and he looks for his wife. She is across the room, a world away, though he can number the steps between them. He hopes she will not forgo their plans for later. The night and its thunderstorm, music, and conversation have suddenly become too much. He needs to separate the room into segments before he can continue: Alice sits on the couch, smiling to herself, aglow; Jane is next to her, laughing at him and his inability to stand up straight; the music plays over their ears, under their feet; and Trevor, his friend, his brother, holds him because he can no longer hold himself. He tells himself to focus, to count the beats in the music. Why did Alice have to sit down on the couch? He saw the way the Jacksons danced, the way they stumbled together. Don't give up hope! Suddenly he feels a racing against his skin. It is Trevor's heart, beating faster than the music, chasing something that will not be outpaced. He worries that Trevor will fall over, but there is no change in their balance. They are still moving, turning in place.

Trevor strokes the back of Allen's head, brushing against the grain of his hairline. Allen is suddenly very drunk, much drunker than any of them conceived. Trevor realizes that if he steps away, even for a brief pause, Allen will topple over, like a newly felled tree. He remembers the water at the bottom of his shirt, his soaked pants. Surely Allen can feel this dampness against his own clothes. Trevor sways to the music, to the song chosen by Jane, whispering in Allen's ear whatever words come to mind. In this embrace, Allen is the vulnerable one, the one ready to collapse, the one lost in drunken reverie. There is an intimacy between them, far greater than the one Trevor has imagined during their runs and conversations at dinner. He is so small, Trevor thinks. Like a kid who has come running. Allen says nothing, but Trevor understands that this is merely part of the dance. His heart begins to race, at first arrhythmically to the music, then in double time. He thinks of an agility drill, how his heart punches against his chest the way two cleats shuffle up and down against the ground. Can Allen feel it? They have never been so close to each other. He looks down, but Allen's eyes are closed, his face clean-shaven and relaxed. He wants his friend to smile, to give some indication that this dance will continue, if not now, then later, when they can acknowledge the current traveling between them, this current they have avoided for years. The music fades. He feels something sink. Tomorrow, he realizes, they will wake up as though nothing has happened.

Allen waits for the music to restart, but Jane has already turned off the stereo. He feels helpless, naked, though Trevor continues to turn them on the floor. Here is another lull. But no, something has changed. The atmosphere isn't the same—this is nothing like a quiet lunch. He pushes Trevor away with a nudge, feeling the cushion of flesh against his knuckles. Did that hurt him? But Trevor is a strong man, capable of picking him up and tossing him in the pool. He looks up. Will Trevor retaliate and shove him back, harder, so his head hits the ground with a thud? But his friend has already returned to his beer. Allen raises his chest.

Alice takes the music stopping as an invitation to leave. It seems that Trevor will not notice her many sighs, the glances at her watch, the quiet pleas she makes with her eyes. She rises from her seat and slips back into her shoes. She will offer to drive and her husband will, of course, refuse. Tonight he has behaved differently, and tomorrow it will take time for her to sort everything out. Instead of rowdy, he has been calm, subdued in a way she doesn't recognize. Maybe it was the mixture of champagne, whiskey, and beer, a cocktail that has tampered with his constitution. Maybe he feels what she felt for that short instant on the couch. She has also seen another side of Allen, the drunk and helpless side. He needs to go lie down and fall asleep. He's had a long day.

Jane lets the Jacksons out of the house, closing the door behind them with a flick of her wrist and swish of her hair. She turns around and walks back into the living room. Her husband is lying on the couch, staring at the ceiling. She watches his eyes widen and shift back and forth under his glasses. "Look who's tired now!" she says.

No more after-party fun for them then. It was unlike him to make plans and not follow through, but he, like she, is exhausted. There is always tomorrow for more celebration in the privacy and comfort of their bedroom. It will be Saturday, which means that she will wake up, still early because of her babies, and nap throughout the day whenever she has the chance.

"Good night," says Jane. "I love you."

Allen closes his eyes without replying, pretending to be asleep. Those words, simple ones spoken thousands of times per day, are different tonight. Tonight they were whispered by someone else.

———————

Matthew Jeffrey Vegari has published fiction in the *Virginia Quarterly Review*, *Boston Review*, and *Epiphany*. He holds an undergraduate degree in English from Harvard College and a master's degree in economics and management from the London School of Economics. He is at work on his first novel.

EDITOR'S NOTE

I was drawn to nominate "The Good, Good Men" because of the complex multivalence of Miles and Theo, the way that Shannon was able to give these two brothers a tenderness not often afforded to black male characters. Shannon's writing, her dialogue especially, felt honest and familiar—not familiar in the sense that I'd heard these voices before, but familiar as if they were kinfolk having a conversation while driving on a road I've been down before. I'm always looking for stories that generate more questions than answers, and Shannon's refusal to provide her reader with a neat/tidy/resolved ending to this family narrative felt exciting for me, and trained my eye to future work from her as a writer. I'm honored that the *Puerto del Sol* Black Voices Series was a first home for her work, and that PEN America is honoring the story now.

Naima Yael Tokunow
Editor, Black Voices Series
Puerto del Sol

THE GOOD, GOOD MEN

Shannon Sanders

THEO HAD COME all the way from New York with no luggage. From the parking lot Miles watched him spring from the train and weave past the other travelers, sidestepping their children and suitcases with practiced finesse, first of anyone to make it across the steaming platform. His hair was shaved close on the sides, one thick strip left to grow skyward from the crown of his head. In his dark, lean clothing, hands shoved deep in his pockets, he was a long streak of black against the brightly colored crowd. He alone had reached their father's full height.

He made no eye contact with Miles as he strode to the car and yanked at the door handle, as he folded himself in half and dropped heavily into the passenger seat, releasing a long breath.

"Fucking hot," he said, pulling the door shut.

Miles threw the car into drive and steered out of the parking lot, out of the knot of station traffic. "Summertime," he said by way of assent.

These words, the first the brothers had spoken aloud to each other in over a year, hung in the air between them until the car reached the mouth of the highway. Their mother, Lee, had finally moved back out to the suburbs, to the end house in a single-family neighborhood Miles had seen often from the road, all crisscrossed with telephone wires. He was grateful for its proximity, only a four-mile drive from the train station. Last time around, searching for her dumpy apartment deep in the District, he and Theo had lost precious time to gridlock and confounding one-way streets and been beaten there by their sisters, turning the whole operation to chaos. A mess of shifted allegiances and hand-wringing, tears, hysteria. Later, in the relative quiet of Miles's living room, Theo had complained of his ears ringing.

"No bag, nothing?" asked Miles now, nodding down toward Theo's empty hands. "We need to stop for a toothbrush?"

"No," said Theo. "I'm good. I'm out tonight, right after Safeway."

Miles thought of Lauren back home, washing the guest linens and googling vegan dinner recipes since morning. "Okay," he said. "Quick trip, though."

"Just to keep it simple," said Theo. "We dragged it out last time. A task like that always expands to fill whatever time you allocate for it. You know? We gave it two days, and it took two days. We were inefficient." He reached for the dashboard and gave the AC knob a hard crank, calling up a blast of chilled air. "This time, two hours. We'll give it two hours, and we'll get it done in two hours."

Miles suppressed a shiver. Stealing a glance at his brother's out-stretched arm, he saw an arc of freshly inked letters at the biceps, disappearing beneath a fitted sleeve. Lauren, who kept aggressive Facebook surveillance of all her in-laws, had kept Miles apprised of each of Theo's new tattoos for years, undeterred by Miles's disinterest. Only this last had caught his attention.

"Bad stakeholder analysis, is what it was," Theo was muttering. "Last time, I mean."

"What's the new tattoo?" asked Miles. "The words on your arm?"

Theo blinked at the graceless transition, then obligingly pushed up his sleeve. "Got it in Los Angeles, on a work trip. A girl I was with talked me into it. I had been thinking about this one for years." He traced his finger around the lettered circle, four words rendered to look like they'd been scrawled on by hand in a familiar chicken scratch. "*Miles, Thelonious, Mariolive, Caprice.* For us, obviously."

"But where did you get Daddy's handwriting to show the tattoo artist?"

Theo let the sleeve drop and folded his arms across his chest. "From a check he sent to the old house for us, with our names in the memo line. I found it in a stack of Lee's work papers with a bunch of other ones and took it when I went to New York. It was in my wallet when I went on the Los Angeles trip."

Miles felt a swell of heat despite the frigid air. "You took a check from her and never gave it back?"

"Did you not hear me? It was with a bunch of other ones, and it was about eight years old. All the checks were years and years old, some of them reissues of older ones—he would write that in the memo line. He would send them, and she would put them some-place idiotic like tucked in the finished crossword puzzles or a pile of old magazines. And then I guess lose them, so he had to write new ones. She was always doing that kind of shit with checks. I found this one, and the others, all mixed in with the girls' old coloring books. I took *one* and left the others there for her to find never. Is that okay with you?"

Theo's posture, now, was rigid, his face turned squarely in the direction of Miles's. Miles took his eyes off the road long enough to stare back, but like a traveler gone too long from his hometown, forgetting its habits and idioms, he had lost his fluency in the quirks of his brother's face. At one time he had been able to tell, from the slightest twitch of an eyelid, that Theo had been teased past his threshold and was about to burst into tears; to hear an impending temper tantrum in the sharpness of his inhalation. All of that was years ago, when any impulse would buzz between them like a current, felt by one brother even before the other acted on it, when a germ passed to either would invade the other in the blink of an eye. A faraway, definitively ended time. The composition of Theo's face was the same as always, brooding features assembled slickly under a strong brow. But now it was like their father's face in the pictures: impassive, all traces of his thoughts as strange and unreadable as hieroglyphics.

LEE HAD A new man, again, this one a fellow patron at the karaoke bar where she'd been throwing away money every week for months. It was known that he mixed good homemade cocktails and spoke a little French, which was probably what had done her in, because he wasn't particularly good-looking and didn't seem like anyone's genius. He had a dog as big as a wolf, supposedly, and for some reason wore too much purple and a signet ring on his little finger.

Miles's spotty intel had come from Mariolive and Caprice, who, working innocently but in tandem, were only a bit less ineffective than either of them was separately. Lauren, for all her expert stalking efforts, couldn't find even a single Facebook reference to supplement what little was known about her mother-in-law's new relationship. It was not known where the new man came from, what he did for a living, or what wives and children lay crumbled in his wake. Nor what in God's name he was doing making regular appearances at karaoke bars, if not trolling for naïfs like Lee.

But without question he had established himself as a regular at Lee's new house out in the suburbs, as evidenced by his car's presence there on each of four spot checks Miles had conducted upon receipt of the intelligence. It was there on a Sunday afternoon, a black sedan parked casually in the carport behind Lee's dented Ford Explorer. There again the following Thursday as Miles inched homeward past the wire-crossed neighborhood in rush-hour traffic. There on a Friday after dark, the lights on in the little house behind it, a hint of movement within. And then, confirming Miles's nauseated suspicions, there again the next morning at sunup, the house still and silent.

Mariolive had said, *At least this one has a car.* Which was more than could be said of certain previous ones, like the one who'd needed Lee to drive him up to Philadelphia once a week to try to see his estranged son. Or the one who'd put the dents in the Ford Explorer driving down 95 in the dark after cocktails.

But still: a grown man, well past any definition of middle age, living unashamedly off a woman with air between her ears. Who lived by the word of her daily horoscope and always kept a tambourine handy to punctuate moments of spontaneous group laughter.

And also: a karaoke bar. An unforgivable fall from grace into the soulless and vulgar. Lee had met their father at a District jazz lounge that no longer existed, a place Miles had long imagined as dark and deliciously moody like the man himself, with threads of light piano melody curling through the air between sets. Their father was the MacHale third of the regular Tuesday-night trio Somebody, Somebody & MacHale (Miles thought he would never forgive Lee for this offense alone, her willful forgetting of the group's full name, which no amount of internet searching could recover), the long-fingered bassist who looked a little like Gil Scott Heron and stood almost as tall as his instrument. MacHale never talked between sets, but he had a smile like a swallow of top-shelf whiskey. Lee had learned from him about melody and improvisation, about modality, how bebop could lift you, how the blues could crush you.

From that she had found her way, albeit over some thirty-five years, into the drunken sump of some suburban karaoke bar. A place where, by very expectation, the music was shit.

Mariolive estimated she'd been hearing consistent mentions of Mr. Signet Ring for two months. Caprice, marginally more reliable in temporal matters, thought it had been four. In his email to Theo, Miles had taken liberties: *Bro. Hope you are well. Yet another motherfucker living up in Lee's house for the past six months. You have time to go to Safeway?*

Theo, perpetually glued to his devices for work purposes, had written back within a minute: *I'll make time. When?*

HE WAS EXPLAINING again about the stakeholder grid. "It's about maximizing your tools to push your agenda forward," he said, drawing squares in the air with long fingers. "You look for the intersection of interest and influence—the people who want what you want and have some power toward achieving it—and you mobilize them. High interest, high influence: that's your first quadrant. That's who you need on your side. They can help you mobilize the folks in the other quadrants. As long as you keep your first quadrant happy, you'll always have some muscle behind your agenda."

"Got it," said Miles.

"My mistake last time," said Theo, "was thinking the girls were in the first quadrant. I thought they were with us and that I could use them that way."

"When really . . . ?"

"*Low* interest, high influence. Not actually on the same page as us, not actually ready to go to goddamn Safeway, but influential. You know? Noisy. They have Lee's ear and she listens to them, wrong as they are. They're third quadrant. You keep third quadrant as far away from the task as possible, because otherwise they'll destroy it."

"Ah."

"Which is why, this time, no girls."

This had been their mistake the last time: inviting their sisters. Mariolive and Caprice were a storm of emotion, almost as changeable and ridiculous as their mother. The last time, when things came to light fisticuffs between Theo and the squatter who had infiltrated Lee's shoebox apartment in the District, both girls had simultaneously burst into hysterical tears. *No, Theo, stop,* they wailed, each one clutching one of Lee's shaking hands. *It's fine, it's fine, just let him stay.* When only days earlier, they'd agreed that the non-rent-paying leech of a boyfriend needed to be escorted out of the too-small apartment. When only minutes earlier, they'd been helping Miles gather the boyfriend's belongings—tattered books, crusted-over cookware—and toss them unscrupulously into the cardboard boxes brought for this purpose. Mariolive had thrown herself in front of the boxes, her thick black braid darting from side to side with each shake of her hair. *Let him stay with Mommy.* Which was why it had taken a total of two days, two trips back to the apartment, two separate escalations of physical contact, to get the lowlife to leave, believably for good.

The time before that: uneventful. The brothers working alone, both of their sisters away at college, had sent the motherfucker packing for Philadelphia within twenty minutes of focused intimidation. Then, as now, Theo had been wearing head-to-toe black, and incidentally Miles had too (he had come straight from coaching football practice), and to the infiltrator they had appeared a powerful and unified posse; the infiltrator—a foot shorter than Theo, who had just reached his full MacHale height at that point—had actually cowered and promised he would never again take advantage of Lee's generosity. Lee herself, crying and wringing her hands in the corner of the room, had been easy to ignore; each brother had a lifetime's practice.

ONCE, MACHALE HAD sent Miles a letter. The letter, etched out in blue ballpoint and in MacHale's erratic, challenging script, confirmed Lee's memory of their first meeting at the long-gone jazz lounge. She had been the girl who turned up to all his gigs in halter dresses she'd made by hand from colorful see-through scarves, swaying her considerable hips at front and center as though they'd hired her as a dancer. Perfect rhythm, and stacked as all hell; but too pretty, an almost unbearable distraction. And too silly to be bothered by the fact that everyone—including MacHale, losing notes on his bass—was watching her. He had never seen anything like her, a black girl with glowing cinnamon skin and hair the color of a well-traveled penny. Sometimes she wore an Afro with a shiny turquoise pick in it, even though by now it was the 1980s and people weren't doing that so much in the District anymore, and on those days he couldn't look at anything but her.

She claimed not to know anything about jazz but somehow could hum all the staple melodies after hearing them once. Often, she brought her own tambourine and accompanied the trio from the lounge floor. The black men and even some of the white ones stared greedily at her, hollering their approval, and even then she didn't stop, her craving for attention apparently bottomless.

I'm sure you know the feeling, read the letter in MacHale's faint handwriting. And even at his first read, Miles *had* known the feeling, having experienced Lee's oblivious attention-seeking many times over, and having also experienced the misery of watching girls he wanted flirt with other men. By instinct he understood why his father had seen no choice but to set aside his bass one day and leave the lounge with her, thirty minutes before the gig was scheduled to end, or to marry her six months later and quit the gig altogether. He certainly didn't need her, the someday mother of his children, swaying and twirling her hips into a future of infinite Tuesday nights.

BELATEDLY, SOMETHING DAWNED on Miles. "Wait," he said. "So you think *I'm* in *your* first quadrant."

Theo, thumbing through emails on his phone, grunted by reply. "If this is done in two hours," he said, "I can get the 7:05 back to New York. There's a gin-tasting event in Brooklyn that I want to get to by midnight."

"Gin at midnight is worth rushing back for?"

"Networking. There's these guys who'll be there that I need to maximize face time with to kick off some new stuff I'm doing in the coding space, and if I hit them up while they're a little bit loose, I might be able to—" He faltered audibly, looked at his brother, and reconsidered. "Anyway, yeah," he concluded finally. "I definitely want to get back for that."

Miles's hand twitched toward the phone in his pocket but instead tightened around the steering wheel. Lauren called this, the type of work people like Theo did in places like Brooklyn, which no amount of description could clarify to outsiders, *alternawork.*

"Unlike Lee," Theo continued, "I can't just leave money on the table. I think about those checks she never cashed, and I just— man." He whistled, a low, pensive sound.

Miles sensed, in the shifts of Theo's upper body, that some familiar, troubled presence had joined them in the car. The mishandling of money had always offended Theo deeply; as a boy, he'd been brought to tears many times by Lee's fretful comments about bills. And from amid the high-piled detritus of the many chintzy apartments Lee had occupied over the years, Theo had somehow sniffed out, and pilfered, MacHale's forgotten child-support checks. There was something so pathetic in it that Miles was almost, *almost* moved to touch his brother's shoulder and to apologize for it, for all of it, on Lee's behalf.

FOR YEARS THE brothers had been inseparable everywhere but at school, where they were two grades apart. Living the other two-thirds of their lives in symbiotic closeness, Miles the mouthpiece for both of them. From playing like the best of friends to fighting savagely at the drop of a hat, their feet and elbows always in each other's face, a constant bodily closeness like nothing Miles would ever experience again. Like a first marriage.

Among other things, MacHale and his wife had argued about

this, whether brothers should be together so much, immersing themselves so fully in their two-person games. Lee had discouraged it, having gotten it into her mind that Miles's engineer's brain was stifling Theo's fanciful imagination, or that they were conspiring daily to rearrange the carefully curated array of crystals and candles on her dresser into an unintelligible mess. She wanted them to be apart sometimes, at least long enough for Miles to complete his early homework assignments without Theo's scribbles winding up all over them. She lived by the importance of occasional aloneness, shutting herself into the bedroom with the crystals for twenty-minute stretches while both boys pawed at the door, indignant.

But in those days she had left them to their own devices for hours while she worked—sometimes impossibly long shifts at the Macy's makeup counter, other times sorting garments at the consignment shop in Northeast, using her pretty face and her honeyed words to sell them to their second owners. Each day, when she was out the door, her long skirts trailing behind her like plumage, MacHale had gathered both boys, not giving a fuck about their aloneness, and sat them before the bass in his practice room to listen while he did his finger warm-ups, his spiderlike scales and arpeggios.

He would play a song or two at a time, then go fix himself a Sazerac, and then do another few songs, delighting the boys by weaving made-up lyrics about Lee into the classics. Into "I Cover the Waterfront" he worked lines about how Lee left her men all home alone too much; "So What" became a song about her big butt and how she wore those skirts to show it off to the men at Macy's.

MacHale gave the boys little nips of his Sazeracs (nasty, and then gradually less nasty) and told them jokes he'd heard at the clubs where sometimes he still played jazz. He disliked television but every so often let them watch episodes of *The Cosby Show*; he sneaked them out to two Spike Lee movies in the space of a year. He said no to buying them a Nintendo, no and no and no again, each of thirty thousand times they asked; but in the afternoons before his gigs, he let them sit on his back to watch cartoons while he snoozed on the couch.

And yes, sometimes he sent them into the master bedroom to swap any two of Lee's crystals, laughing riotously and giving them double high fives when they returned triumphant.

And then Lee, returning late at night from doing inventory at the consignment shop, was a wildcard who often shattered the consistent peace of daytime. She might be happy and pull out her tambourine, shaking it and her hips when the whole family was laughing. But she might just as readily make a beeline for the stove and wordlessly slam a pan onto it, storm clouds nearly visible over her slick copper-colored bun as she began to stir-fry chicken and peppers. MacHale making the boys laugh by mimicking her cooking posture with exaggerated flourishes, or pretending to bite the nape of her bare neck like a vampire.

Her high drama, her hysterical turns of phrase. *Tell it to the devil, you piece of shit,* Miles once heard her scream on the front porch under his bedroom window, the words slicing their way into his dream. Her idea of a welcome-home as MacHale returned from one of the many gigs that didn't end till well past midnight. She ranted with wild passion, her words otherwise shrill and indistinct, while MacHale responded at a blessedly normal volume, his low, moody murmur so comforting that before he knew it Miles had drifted back to sleep. In the morning it was as though nothing had happened; she served the boys their eggs and toast with a wide artificial smile, pretty as ever with a purple ribbon braided into her hair.

———

AT ONE OF these gigs, MacHale broke his left tibia and fibula and
landed himself in the hospital for a stay that dragged on like a
prison sentence, forcing Lee to quit the Macy's job and surrender
several of her shifts at the consignment shop. (*Are we going to be
poor?* Theo asked, practically in tears; and Lee laughed one of her
untamed, destabilizing laughs. *You thought we were rich before
this?*)

After that MacHale was on the couch, suffering the television
he so disliked with his leg stretched stiff before him, eating half of
what Lee offered him and rejecting the other half, irritable each
time she reminded him he could not drink whiskey—not even in
cocktail form—on meds as strong as the ones he'd been prescribed.

She was moving more slowly than usual, in the first bloom of
visible pregnancy with the girls, and she complained often about
her aching back and feet in a way that seemed to Miles to be wildly
insensitive, considering. MacHale called the boys to him on a
Saturday morning. *We need eggs and sausage and green onions*, he
said, making eye contact first with Miles, then with Theo, looking
back and forth between them; nothing he had ever told them had
seemed so important. *But I don't like your mama swishing around
in the streets like she does. You boys go with Lee to Safeway and
you don't let nothing happen to her. Nobody looking funny at her,
nothing. You understand?*

The boys, with their small chests puffed out, gangly Theo actually walking on tiptoe to appear taller, flanked her dutifully on the
walk to Safeway.

The eggs were found easily, but in an aisle full of loitering men,
so Theo stayed behind with Lee while Miles darted ahead and

grabbed a carton, checking the contents for cracks as he'd been shown to do.

Aren't you helpful, said Lee.

She forgot her purse in the aisle with the sausage but didn't realize it till they'd reached the green onions five aisles over; Miles, able to see in his memory's eye the maroon felt satchel slung over one of the shelves, deployed Theo back to that aisle, holding Lee in place with produce-related questions until his brother returned triumphant with the purse.

In the checkout line they stood behind Lee, shoulder to shoulder between her and the other customers, because she was wearing one of those skirts and it just seemed like the thing to do.

At home, their chests puffed out ever farther, they each received praise and a kiss to the forehead from MacHale, and the pride that hummed between them nearly overpowered Miles's eight-year-old body.

A week later, wobbling a bit on his new crutches, MacHale took his sons to the toy store and led them straight up to the checkout counter, behind which was kept all the costliest merchandise. With each hand palming one of his sons' flocked heads, MacHale got the cashier's attention and nodded up to the top shelf.

A—what do you call it, Miles? A Super Nintendo Entertainment System, please. We'll take one of those for these good, good boys.

Happiness hummed between Miles and Theo, their feelings in perfect alignment, one of the last moments in which this would ever occur.

Some weeks after that, MacHale recovered the ability to walk without crutches, and then he was gone, driven away finally by Lee's whims and her nattering.

———

THIRTEEN YEARS LATER, Miles would break his left tibia and fibula playing college football and find himself bedridden for too long and slowed by a cast for even longer, a total of six idle weeks during which he thought he might scratch out his own eyeballs from boredom. When the cast came off, he would feel as though he'd been fired from a cannon, an unstoppable projectile who ran instead of walked whenever possible, and through this experience come to understand finally why after surviving all those years with Lee his father nonetheless could not survive a single solitary second with her post-crutches.

And sometime thereafter, when MacHale's letter, five dense handwritten pages addressed "To my firstborn on his twenty-first birthday"—only a few weeks late—arrived to confirm the projectile theory, Miles would find that he felt satisfied with this explanation. Not that he had ever felt particularly otherwise.

BUT IN THE immediate, MacHale's abrupt exit ripped a hole in their little house in Northeast, all its inhabitants left at Lee's mercy. What outcome could MacHale possibly have foreseen but pandemonium? Before anything else, there was Lee's unilaterally scrapping Ella and Pearl, the very good names MacHale had chosen for his daughters-to-be, replacing them with absurdities she'd dreamed up through God only knew what nutty arithmancy. There was an intolerable glut of visitors, relatives of Lee's come out of the woodwork to rock the babies and distract Miles and Theo from their grief with nonsensical questions about school. There were foods served that MacHale never would have tolerated, the delicious staples replaced with egg-plant and tofu and loaves of bread with pea-size seeds in them.

There was the unceremonious discarding of the double bass, which MacHale had said he would come back for but which instead became the property of a disadvantaged District high school's mu-sic department. MacHale's left-behind shirts and pants, the ones he wore to gigs, a spare collection of twenty or so all-black garments, were swept from the master closet and sent to the Salvation Army. MacHale's Copper Pony went down the toilet and the bottles into the trash can, leaving the bar cart empty. For a short time they lived as in a sanitarium, every word anyone spoke echoing disconcert-ingly off the bare walls.

It did not last. Soon enough Lee filled the closet with more clothes of her own; the extra space seemed to give her the feel-ing that she could now acquire as many impractical garments as she wanted, new things from department stores and all the left-over inventory from the consignment shop. Bolts of cloth found all over the place, wrapped around her body in ridiculous ways but still drawing street whistles that burned her sons' ears. She be-gan wearing her turquoise Afro pick again, sometimes in her hair, sometimes tied to a length of cord and worn above her cleavage as a statement necklace. She spray-painted the bar cart magenta and gold and filled the top half with the priciest of each kind of spirit, the bottom with bottles of wine brought to the house by her consignment-shop employees and other friends when they visited.

She collected stacks of papers that nearly reached the ceilings. Recipes torn from health magazines; drawings the girls did that she could not bear to throw away; Miles's and Theo's schoolwork, which miraculously had not lapsed. When mail arrived bearing MacHale's name, she quickly spirited it away, envelopes and all, to places unseen, sometimes returning the most boring contents—old invoices, typewritten correspondence from the city—to her stacks of papers. Lee's treatment of MacHale's more personal mail infuriated Miles: sometimes he'd see the scraps of ripped-up letters in the trash can and want to explode.

Once she opened a check from MacHale and laughed aloud as she crumpled it into a ball before Miles's horrified eyes.

If I threw this on the ground, it would bounce right through the ceiling, she said with a cackle, dropping it into the pocket of her carnelian skirt.

There was no more jazz; she played terrible music on the tape player and then on the CD player, and cheered the children through their homework with that imbecilic tambourine.

Look what I found! she crowed one day, and to Miles's horror she pulled from her satchel two sets of hand cymbals to give her daughters. Their small hands barely fit into the straps, but they screamed with happiness anyway, filling the room with noise.

SHE GAVE MACHALE'S entire vinyl collection to a man she met at work, and for the first time in a while Miles and Theo had something to talk about.

She gave Daddy's records to that guy, said Miles, barging into Theo's room and finding him there with his head in a textbook. *I think they might be dating or something.*

Theo lifted his head, looking sick. *Oh, that's nasty,* he said.

A silence hung between them. After a time, Miles cleared his throat. *Do you ever,* he asked carefully, *think about that one time when Daddy sent us with her to Safeway?*

And then bought us the Nintendo.

Yeah.

Yeah.

MILES HAD DECIDED immediately upon receipt of MacHale's only letter to him that he would neither mention nor show it to Theo. It went on for five pages and did not once mention MacHale's younger son, nor either of his daughters. The return address, to which Miles sent multiple overeager replies, had turned over to another renter mere days earlier, with no hints as to where MacHale might have gone. Anyway, the letter itself was more than good enough, even the revelation of seeing MacHale's quirky handwriting up close an unexpected joy. Whatever unease he had felt seeing it inked on Theo's arm was repaired by knowing its less-than-honorable origins.

Their exit loomed. "Will Lauren and I see you again soon, then?" asked Miles, flicking on his turn signal.

"Don't know," said Theo.

Miles thought of Mariolive, who by Lauren's report was holding on to her shithead college boyfriend even though she should know better by now, all those letters after her name. Maybe they'd be hitting Safeway again soon, for her.

Into the shabby, wire-crossed neighborhood, he steered the car. Beside him, Theo was silent but alert, scanning the boxy little houses of Lee's neighbors, his phone inert in his pocket.

The grass was freshly cut, a touch that struck Miles as the work of a much craftier adversary than all the sloppy past boyfriends. A dog, chained to Lee's wrought-iron fence and unsurprisingly not wolf-size, slept under Mr. Signet Ring's black sedan. Its collar was turquoise and spattered with glitter and seemed to have sprouted a number of multicolored feathers.

They retrieved the cardboard boxes from the trunk and walked shoulder to shoulder up the walkway, Theo hunching just the tiniest, barely perceptible bit, which Miles appreciated. A hideous summer foliage wreath hung from the front door, and the faintest four-on-the-floor seemed to pulse through a downstairs window.

Both brothers lifted their fists. Theo dropped his, and Miles knocked.

Lee herself opened the door, a fuchsia scarf tied around her silver-and-copper hair. The synthesized sounds of disco music flooded out into the front yard, rousing the dog. Shades of excitement and then concern passed over her expressive face in an instant. "Boys?"

Behind her, sitting on the couch in veritable purple jeans, the *Post* spread out before him, his ringed little finger keeping time against the edge of the newspaper, sat Mr. Signet Ring himself, looking at the brothers with only mild curiosity.

"You," said Theo, maintaining eye contact with the boyfriend as he stepped around his mother, while Miles began the work of containing her in the foyer. "We need to talk to you."

Shannon Sanders is a Black writer and attorney, and a graduate of Spelman College and Georgetown University Law Center. Her fiction appears in *One Story*, Electric Literature's *The Commuter*, *SLICE*, *Strange Horizons*, *Joyland*, and elsewhere. She was a 2019 finalist for *One Story*'s Adina Talve-Goodman Fellowship and has placed in *Glimmer Train*'s Very Short Fiction Award contest. Find her at ShannonSandersWrites.com, on Twitter @ShandersWrites, and on Instagram @i.exaggerate.

ABOUT THE JUDGES

TRACY O'NEILL is the author of the novels *The Hopeful* and *Quotients*. She has been named a National Book Foundation 5 Under 35 honoree and awarded the Center for Fiction's Emerging Writer Fellowship. Her writing has appeared in *Granta*, *Rolling Stone*, *The Atlantic*, *The New Yorker*, and *VQR*. She attended the MFA program at CCNY and the PhD program in communications at Columbia University.

NAFISSA THOMPSON-SPIRES is the author of *Heads of the Colored People*, which won the PEN Open Book Award, the Los Angeles Times Art Seidenbaum Award for First Fiction, the Hurston/Wright Legacy Award, and an Audie Award. She is also the recipient of a 2019 Whiting Award. Her work has appeared in *The Paris Review Daily*, *Dissent*, and *BuzzFeed Books*. She teaches creative writing at Cornell University.

DEB OLIN UNFERTH is the author of six books, most recently the novel *Barn 8*. Her work has appeared in *Harper's Magazine*, *The Paris Review*, *Granta*, *VICE*, *Tin House*, *The New York Times*, *NOON*, and *McSweeney's*. An associate professor at the University of Texas at Austin, she has received a Guggenheim Fellowship, three Pushcart Prizes, and was a finalist for the National Book Critics' Circle Award. She also teaches creative writing at a penitentiary in southern Texas.

ABOUT THE PEN/ ROBERT J. DAU SHORT STORY PRIZE FOR EMERGING WRITERS

THE PEN/ROBERT J. Dau Short Story Prize for Emerging Writers recognizes twelve fiction writers for a debut short story published in a print or online literary magazine. The annual award was offered for the first time during PEN America's 2017 Literary Awards cycle.

The twelve winning stories are selected by a committee of three judges. The writers of the stories each receives a two-thousand-dollar cash prize and is honored at the annual PEN America Literary Awards Ceremony in New York City. Every year, Catapult will publish the winning stories in *Best Debut Short Stories: The PEN America Dau Prize.*

This award is generously supported by the family of the late Robert J. Dau, whose commitment to the literary arts has made him a fitting namesake for this career-launching prize. Mr. Dau was born and raised in Petoskey, a city in northern Michigan in close proximity to Walloon Lake, where Ernest Hemingway had spent his summers as a young boy and which serves as the backdrop for Hemingway's *The Torrents of Spring.* Petoskey is also known for being where Hemingway determined that he would commit to becoming a writer. This proximity to literary history ignited the Dau family's interest in promoting emerging voices in fiction and spotlighting the next great fiction writer.

LIST OF PARTICIPATING PUBLICATIONS

PEN America and Catapult gratefully acknowledge the following publications, which published debut fiction in 2019 and submitted work for consideration to the PEN/Robert J. Dau Short Story Prize.

805 Lit + Art
Alaska Quarterly Review
American Literary Review
Anomaly
Apogee Journal
The Bare Life Review
Barrelhouse
Belmont Story Review
Black Warrior Review
bluestockings magazine
Boston Review
Cagibi
Carve
Chicago Quarterly Review
The Cincinnati Review
Conjunctions
CRAFT
Cricket
Deep Overstock
deLuge
Doek!
Driftwood Press
Dryland
Emrys Journal

The Fiddlehead
F(r)iction
Foglifter Journal
Granta
Into the Void
Hawaii Pacific Review
Hot Metal Bridge
The Iowa Review
Jelly Bucket
Lady Churchill's Rosebud Wristlet
The Literary Review
The London Reader
The Meadow
Menacing Hedge
Michigan Quarterly Review
Mount Hope
New England Review
The New Guard
New Ohio Review
October Hill Magazine
Orca, a Literary Journal
Outlook Springs
Oyster River Pages
Paper Darts
The Paris Review
Puerto del Sol
Quarterly West
The Rumpus
The Rupture
Scribble

So to Speak Journal
The Summerset Review
The Threepenny Review
Trouble Child
Vestal Review
Washington Square Review
The Write Launch
ZYZZYVA

PERMISSIONS

"Bat Outta Hell" by Damitri Martinez. First published in *Foglifter* 4, no. 1 (April, 2019). Copyright © Damitri Martinez. Reprinted by permission of the author.

"Cats vs. Cancer" by Valerie Hegarty. First published in *New England Review* 40, no. 1 (March 2019). Copyright © Valerie Hegarty. Reprinted by permission of the author.

"Dog Dreams" by Sena Moon. First published in *Quarterly West*, no. 97 (2019). Copyright © Sena Moon. Reprinted by permission of the author.

"Don't Go to Strangers" by Matthew Jeffrey Vegari. First published in *ZYZZYVA* 35, no. 115 (April 2019). Copyright © Matthew Jeffrey Vegari. Reprinted by permission of the author.

"Evangelina Concepcion" by Ani Cooney. First published in *Epiphany* 15th Anniversary Issue (Spring/Summer 2019). Copyright © Ani Cooney. Reprinted by permission of the author.

"Failure to Thrive" by Willa C. Richards. First published in *The Paris Review* no. 231 (Winter 2019). Copyright © Willa C. Richards. Reprinted by permission of the author.

PEN America stands at the intersection of literature and human rights to protect free expression in the United States and worldwide. The organization champions the freedom to write, recognizing the power of the word to transform the world. Its mission is to unite writers and their allies to celebrate creative expression and defend the liberties that make it possible. Learn more at PEN.org.